MONKEY'S WEDDING

D0071747

MONKEY'S WEDDING

Rossandra White

ISBN 978-0-9985949-0-3

First Edition

Cover design by Teddi Black
Interior design by Megan McCullough

*For my brother Garth (the inspiration for Jiminy),
who has been waiting ever so patiently for the
publication of Monkey's Wedding*

A friend is someone you share the path with.
~ African proverb

Contents

Chapter 1 1

Chapter 2 9

Chapter 3 21

Chapter 4 29

Chapter 5 35

Chapter 6 45

Chapter 7 49

Chapter 8 59

Chapter 9 65

Chapter 10 71

Chapter 11 81

Chapter 12 91

Chapter 13 99

Chapter 14 105

Chapter 15 115

Chapter 16 123

Chapter 17 131

Chapter 18 145

Chapter 19 149

Chapter 20 153

Chapter 21 161

Chapter 22 167

Chapter 23 171

Chapter 1

Southern Rhodesia, a British protectorate
Friday, August 7, 1953

THE JACKAL TUGGED ON THE BODY IT HAD UNCOVERED behind the beer hall, its jaws locked around a bloody, dirt-encrusted forearm. A short distance away, a hyena lowered its head and edged forward. The jackal stopped, eyed the hyena, and howled a warning.

Two miles away on the Bradley sisal plantation, Elizabeth McKenzie, on her knees beside a muddy flower bed, heard the howl and stopped digging. The only sound was the rustle of the swordlike leaves of the surrounding fields of sisal plants. Then the jackal howled again. She gave a shiver and glanced toward the house, taking comfort from the light in the kitchen where their houseboy, Nelson, was already at work.

Nudging her long, tangled hair away from her face with the back of one dirty hand, she gripped the end of a wooden spoon with the other and dragged it down the length of the flower bed. She sat back and eyed the results, then tore open the packet of sweet pea seeds she'd slipped from her mother's gardening box and sprinkled them down the rut. A strip of chicken wire she'd molded to cover and protect them from the chickens lay nearby.

She was still in her pajamas, although she was wearing a jersey against the early-morning chill of the cold season. She had slipped from the house before anyone else was up. She rarely slept past dawn, afraid she might miss something. Even though there was never anything to miss. Still, these days, there was another reason to get out of the house: her mother was going to have a baby, and it was making her more and more high-strung by the minute. And she still had two months to go. Elizabeth planned on surprising her by planting the sweet pea seeds, her favorite flower.

Pookie, Elizabeth's pet bantam chicken, appeared from behind an overturned wheelbarrow a few yards away, pecking at the ground. A runt, Pookie had never grown all her feathers, except for those on her legs, which made it look like she was wearing little flared brown skirts. Pookie stopped mid-peck, eyed the sweet pea seeds, then shot toward the flower bed like a shuttlecock whacked across a badminton net.

"No!" Elizabeth jammed the protective cover over the seeds.

Pookie stared down through the wire for a moment, then shifted and took a stab at the seed packet. It crackled and she jumped, feather skirts quivering. Elizabeth laughed and stroked Pookie's moth-eaten head. The bird held still for a moment and then, clucking nervously, pecked her way back toward the chicken coop.

Elizabeth sighed. She wished Pookie would allow a nice, tight hug now and then, like a puppy would. In fact, she wished Pookie were a puppy. But every time she asked for one, her mother said no. Well, at least there was the baby coming. She couldn't wait to play with him. And a him it would be. It had to be. Her mother couldn't take another girl.

Angry voices burst from the house, and her stomach clenched. Her parents were arguing again. The back door burst open and her father, Mac, flew down the steps and hurried toward their Ford, which looked like a black bathtub turned upside down.

She scrambled to her feet. "Daddy!" The slamming of the screen door drowned out her voice.

She watched helplessly as her father reversed down the rut of a driveway, swung left, and in a cloud of red dust, tore down the dirt road toward the sisal-curing sheds. Why was he headed to work on his day off? What about the breakfast they were supposed to share?

"Missi."

Elizabeth turned. "Turu!"

Nelson's son, Tururu, stood yawning and stretching in the doorway of the *kiya*—the servants' quarters—he shared with his father, his cast-off shorts and shirt wrinkled with sleep.

"Shh!" He lifted his chin in the direction of the house. He didn't want Nelson to hear them and make Turu help him in the kitchen.

"I thought you'd already gone to your grandmother's," she whispered. Every Saturday, he apprenticed with his witch doctor grandmother. "So can you play, then?"

He shook his head. "Grandmother is waiting."

She tried to hide her disappointment. It wasn't a good idea to let the servants think you cared. It made them expect things and lose respect for you. Or so her mother always said.

"Will Karari be there?"

He nodded. "Karari will be *godobori*."

"*He's* going to be the next big witch doctor? I thought you were."

He gave a sharp shake of his head.

"Well, how am I supposed to know, what with all those lessons you're taking? Anyway, you really shouldn't be seen with him. My dad says he's a troublemaker. Especially not now with this whole federation fuss going on."

Britain's law uniting Southern Rhodesia and its two neighboring countries was about to go into effect. The blacks hadn't been given a vote, and a lot of them were upset over it.

He gave a half shrug.

"Everybody thinks you're all going to riot, you know," she said.

She hoped he'd protest, tell her they would never do such a thing. Instead, he turned his head at the sound of a voice inside the *kiya*. His mother, Dakarai. This was one of the weekends she visited from their village, a couple of miles to the east, near the beer hall. He disappeared for a moment.

The screen door squealed, and Nelson emerged from the house. He pulled a *stompie*, a blackened, hand-rolled cigarette stub, from his top pocket and started down the back steps. Turu charged from the *kiya* and headed for the lane at the back of the yard. Elizabeth ducked behind the wheelbarrow and peered through a hole at Nelson. She didn't like him. He was nasty and always whacking Turu behind the head for nothing.

Nelson stopped, stuck the *stompie* into his mouth and, with a quick flick of a match against the bottom of his shoe, lit the end and inhaled.

"*Picannin* missus," he called through a stream of smoke.

Elizabeth stayed put.

Rocking on his heels, Nelson blew smoke rings in the air. The damp cold of the ground seeped into Elizabeth's bones, and she shivered.

Enough of this. Pretending he wasn't there, she strolled back toward the sweet pea bed.

"Eh, missus. I call you."

"What do you want?" she called over her shoulder.

He didn't answer. She glanced back.

Nelson was staring up at a hawk eagle making lazy circles in the sky, its familiar black-and-white underfeathers a sharp contrast against the blue. She glanced around the yard for Pookie. She'd already lost one pet chicken to one of those birds. There was no sign of the bantam. In the coop, she hoped.

Nelson's gaze shifted to the overgrown patch at the bottom of the yard.

"What are you looking at?" she asked, following his gaze.

He stared blankly at her for a moment. "Where is medem's spoon?"

She shrugged.

He glared at her. "Medem's spoon."

Elizabeth hesitated just long enough to let him know he couldn't boss her around, retrieved the spoon, and strolled back toward him. Nelson took one last draw of his *stompie*, pinched the lit end between thumb and forefinger, stuffed the remains into his pocket, and held out his hand.

Elizabeth gave a small shudder. Even though she'd been told Africans didn't feel pain like whites did, she just knew putting out a cigarette like that had to hurt. Holding out the spoon like she was in a relay race, she let him take it from her as she marched past.

He frowned at its muddy state. "Medem not like this."

"She doesn't mind, so there." She skipped up the steps into the house.

Sounds of retching greeted her. Her mother, Annie, was at it again. Remembering she was still in her pajamas, she hurried toward her bedroom.

Her mother emerged from the bathroom, wiping her face with a wet washcloth. "Hold on right there. What have I told you about running around outside half-naked?"

Elizabeth made a show of looking down at herself. "Half-naked?"

"Don't you get cheeky with me, young lady. I've told you before, it doesn't take much to arouse those *kaffirs*. And with what's been happening, well, I don't want to even think about it."

Elizabeth opened her mouth to argue but closed it again.

"It's just that I worry about you," her mother continued, her voice quavering. "Girls are so vulnerable in this world, especially at your—"

"I planted sweet peas for you."

Her mother blew her nose on the washcloth. "That's nice."

Elizabeth sighed. So much for her big surprise. "Well, I'd better go get dressed then."

"Wait a minute." Reaching out, her mother lifted a lock of Elizabeth's hair. "When was the last time you brushed this bird's nest? I mean really got stuck in, not just waved the brush over it."

"Yesterday."

"I don't believe it. Get in there." She nodded toward the master bedroom. "It's time for a thorough combing."

Elizabeth groaned. "I can do it myself, honestly."

"Not another word. Sit."

Elizabeth slumped onto the padded, kidney-shaped stool in front of her mother's dressing table and scowled into the mirror. Her mother lifted a handful of Elizabeth's long, tawny hair and began to tug a comb through it.

"Ow!"

"I should just cut it all off right now, like a boy's, and be done with the aggravation."

Gritting her teeth, Elizabeth hunched over. After the first few knots were combed through, it didn't hurt that much. A couple of times her mother stopped and, with a wince, pressed a hand against her belly. The baby. Her eyes strayed to her mother's stomach. To think an entire human being was lying in there, growing fingers and toes and elbows and knees and a heart and everything. And it got there because her parents had done "it." She colored at the thought.

Her mother stopped combing. "What on earth's the matter with you?"

Elizabeth felt her face blaze anew. "Um, nothing."

"You're not getting sick, are you?"

"Medem." Nelson stood behind them, holding a tea tray.

Her mother gave a start and swung around. "We'll take our tea in the kitchen. Thank you, Nelson."

"Yes, medem." He turned and left the room.

"See what I mean?" her mother said in a low voice. "He didn't even knock. Besides, he knows I don't like him in here before I'm dressed. I'm telling you, they're getting bolder by the minute."

"He's always nasty to Turu, you know."

"That's different. Hand me the brush."

Bending to the task, her mother brushed Elizabeth's hair until it gleamed and then plaited a single thick tress down her back.

"I wish you wouldn't make it so tight." Elizabeth clasped her head between both hands. "I can hardly see where I'm going when you're done."

"Nonsense." Her mother wove a yellow ribbon into the last few inches. "I want you to keep it braided from now on; you've got some nasty split ends. I'll trim them next week. Oh, and before I forget, you need to try on that blue dress so I can finish it. I want you to wear it when Mr. Coetzee comes on Monday."

"No lessons on Monday." Elizabeth rubbed her temples where the hair stretched her skin. "It's Federation Day, remember?"

"Wear it on Wednesday, then. The point is I want you to start dressing like a young lady."

"I don't want to get all dressed up just for Mr. Coetzee. He doesn't care what I'm wearing."

"With boarding school coming up, you need to get into the habit of wearing something other than shorts and a blouse."

Boarding school. That whole nightmare. She slipped off the stool and started for the door but then stopped. "Why did Daddy go to work today? He told me he didn't have to."

Her mother didn't look up from combing hair from the brush. "He wanted to check on a machine that's been acting up."

"But what about driving Mrs. B. to the station?"

"Oh, I'm sure he'll be back in time for that," her mother said, a note of bitterness in her voice. She looked up, and their eyes met in the mirror. "Listen, Bitty, when your little brother is born, you can help me change his diaper and bathe him. All right?"

Elizabeth grinned and nodded.

Shoveling a spoonful of porridge into her mouth, Elizabeth watched an ant carry a grain of sugar across the gingham-patterned oilcloth covering the old wooden kitchen table Mrs. Bradley gave them when she got her new Formica one. Nelson stood at the sink, scouring a pot.

"Nelson, why do they call them Matabele ants?"

He didn't answer.

"Bwana Coetzee says that a long time ago, Chief Lobengula brought his people up here from South Africa. That's how the Matabele tribe got here, you know, and actually the Shona too." She grinned. "Anyway, why do you think they call them Matabele ants and not Shona ants?"

He kept working on the pot.

Nelson had no sense of humor at all. "Well?"

"Nelson not Matabele."

"What's that got to do with it?"

He turned and glared at her. "Finish porridge."

"I'm almost finished, can't you see?"

He poured milk into a glass, ambled over, and thumped it on the table in front of her. Milk splashed onto the oilcloth.

"That's very disrespectful. I'm going to tell madam!"

Whipping the dishtowel from his shoulder, he mopped the milk away with a hard swipe, all the while glaring at her.

"That cloth is only for drying dishes," she said. "Honestly."

Making a sharp, dismissive clicking sound with his tongue, Nelson flicked the towel back over his shoulder and headed toward the back door.

Elizabeth drained her milk. The kitchen cabinet's top compartment was open. It was usually locked to keep Elizabeth from swiping guests-only ladyfinger biscuits—and also to prevent Nelson from helping himself to cigarettes and sugar. With a glance toward her mother's bedroom, she hopped onto the cabinet's wooden ledge and removed two biscuits. Stuffing them into her shorts pocket, she jumped down.

"What *picannin* missus doing?" Propped against the doorjamb, Nelson looked her up and down, a smirk on his face.

Elizabeth gave a start. "Nothing."

He snorted.

Elizabeth turned and strolled toward her bedroom, but her heart was pounding. Her mom was right. They were getting bolder.

Chapter 2

TURURU FOLLOWED HIS GRANDMOTHER, ANESU, SHONA high priestess, to the great god Zane's shrine in the ancient ruins of their people. Dogged by his usual nervousness at what they had to do, he lugged a basket filled with brushwood, dried herbs, and a small leather pouch containing magic powder. Red dust motes danced in the early morning sunlight pouring through the crumbling walls. This was where his grandmother cast her spells to rid the valley of the whites—the same magic her people had used in ancient times to chase away their enemies.

She'd started the ritual right after bwana Bradley arrived, five years earlier. He stood for all the years when their land hadn't been restored to them, even as they patiently waited. Tururu didn't mind getting rid of the whites—well, except for Missi Elizabeth. But he had something else to worry about lately. Amai Vedu Africa, the Great Mother, had come to his grandmother in a vision and told her Tururu was to become *n'anga*, a maker of spells and healer to his people.

"B-but I am Tururu," he'd said when Grandmother told him.

His nickname wasn't "mouse" for nothing. How could someone who wasn't very brave, who sometimes stammered, be *n'anga*? He felt he was much better suited to making toys out of wire scraps.

"Amai Vedu knows all," she'd said, but she had looked worried as well.

Well, at least *he* was not to become *godobori*. That took courage and cleverness. His grandmother had chosen Karari for that task. He had the makings of a powerful *godobori*, she said, clever in so many ways, cunning and incorruptible by the whites—an almost worthy successor to her. Despite his temper.

Grandmother stopped and lifted her chin, like an antelope sniffing the air for predators. Her right eye shimmered, the one that had been clouded over since birth. She was gazing into the spirit world. "There *is* a dead body on the veld," she whispered.

Tururu felt a twinge of alarm. Dead bodies showed up now and then on the veld, some victim of a drunken fight or someone with a grudge. But this one felt different. Even he could feel that.

Grandmother twisted her head this way and that, as if to refocus. Tururu drew closer in case she breathed a name, for she wouldn't remember it later. Instead, she stopped and reached for her magic amulet, a small, green soapstone bird she usually wore around her neck.

"*Nadira* is back at the hut," Tururu said. This is what he did best—kept track of Grandmother's possessions. She could be absent-minded sometimes.

She frowned and stared off into the distance. And then, as if coming to, she turned to him. "What are you waiting for?"

Tururu hurried through the entrance to the inner chamber and the circle of rocks in the center, dropped to his knees, and began stacking the kindling. Gathering up her great skirts, Grandmother eased down onto her knees with a grunt. She closed her eyes and sat still as a rock, then lifted her chin and uttered an incantation.

The air vibrated.

Opening her eyes, she jabbed her forefinger toward the firewood. It crackled and burst into blue-tinged flames with hearts of brilliant orange. *Ngozi*. Fire beings from the center of the earth, children of Gurutu, Goddess of the Underworld. Tururu turned away from their mesmerizing brilliance.

It took a great *godobori* like Grandmother to call up and order about these fire spirits. For the weak or less experienced, the *ngozi* were the ones who took control. These beings kept the fire in front of Grandmother's hut burning, day and night, providing heat for cooking and keeping her hut warm on cold winter nights. She also used their power in some of her magic ceremonies.

Grandmother reached for her magic pouch, withdrew a handful of black-speckled powder, and threw it on the blaze. The *ngozi* flared for a moment in a show of blue brilliance but then, murmuring and hissing, they settled back down again.

In a voice as strong and deep as thunder, Grandmother spoke: "Oh, great Gurutu, on this your day, Anesu comes to ask for your help to rid our land of the white jackals."

She clapped her hands three times and uttered a stream of incantations. Sneaking a glance at the fire, Tururu wished he'd paid more attention to the meaning of the ancient words. As Grandmother spoke the fire began to die, but not without a hiss and a luminous flare here and there as the *ngozi* fought to remain. Soon all that was left was an unnatural glow in the center of the circle.

Grandmother let out a deep, throaty hum. The earth vibrated around them as if to join in. Dirt showered down from the ancient walls. The Goddess had heard her.

Grandmother sat back with chin lifted and arms outstretched toward the heavens for a couple of moments before struggling to her feet.

Tururu gathered everything and replaced it in the basket. Now they had to hurry across the veld before the *tokoloshi*—those mischievous elemental dwellers of the underworld—rose from beneath the earth, drawn by the strong magic. These small creatures could create terrible destruction by gouging out eyes, raping women, and biting off sleeping people's toes. That was why everyone raised their beds with three feet of bricks. Grandmother wasn't afraid of them, but they were always after Tururu.

Tururu let his grandmother lead the way again. He hadn't gone ten yards beyond the temple entrance before a hairy claw reached up through the earth and tried to grab his foot. He shrieked and jumped back.

Grandmother whirled around and jabbed a stiffened finger toward it. Sparks flew from her finger, and the apparition curled up like a strip of bacon on a hot pan and disappeared back into the ground.

Tururu charged up beside her, almost tripping them both. "Aiyee."

"Come-come, Tururu," Grandmother said. "What have I told you about being strong inside? *Tokoloshi* smell fear. Did you do the protection work I taught you?"

"Uh . . ."

She clucked her tongue and continued walking. "Grandmother will not always be here to protect you."

"Yes, G-grandmother." He stayed as close to her as possible and glanced around for the small creatures.

"Amai Vedu has chosen you to be *n'anga*, and she does not choose poorly. You have the power in your heart, but you must believe in yourself. And if you do not use the power in your heart, it will be hard. Very hard. You could become a bad *n'anga*. But Tururu is not a bad boy."

"Tururu shall have *ngozi* eternal fire, like Grandmother?"

"Yes, yes. But first you must learn how to control the *ngozi*."

"Father says—"

Grandmother stopped and turned to face him, her eyes hard. "That I have eternal fire because I serve *ngozi*?"

"Uh . . ." He bit his lip. What possessed him to bring up his father? Why couldn't he keep his thoughts to himself?

"What does your father say?"

"Um, he s-say *tokoloshi*—"

"That *tokoloshi* is husband to Grandmother?"

He studied his toes.

She clucked her tongue and took off—at a fast clip for such a large woman. Tururu chased after her.

"What a stupid, stupid man," she continued. "How could Dakarai have chosen such a fool? The only thing Nelson has done well is father you."

She stopped as if she'd run into a wall, then cocked her head. Tururu almost ran into her. "We have to go. Quickly," she said.

In the next moment, she had him by the hand and was muttering an incantation. He knew what was coming. He clutched the basket to his chest.

It was like being pulled through water and flying at the same time. It always made his ears pop and his insides swoop up into his mouth. And then he was standing inside the cool depths of Grandmother's hut. Just like that. It never failed to surprise him how it happened. No landing. Just standing there on the hard-packed dirt floor, his hand still in Grandmother's and his head spinning a little.

He glanced around, wondering what had alerted her.

Karari!

The man stood beside Grandmother's trunk, holding an old, scarred box in one hand. Her magic soapstone bird dangled from his other hand. How had he gotten past the protective magic ring around Grandmother's hut?

Karari's head snapped up, and he dropped the box. It hit the dirt floor with a dull thud.

"You would dare touch *nadira!*" Grandmother snatched the amulet from his fingers with one hand and struck him across the face with the back of the other.

Karari spun around with the force of the blow and stumbled sideways. Tururu saw temper flare in his eyes, but then he seemed to compose himself. He drew himself up and turned to face Grandmother. "It is time for my own amulet."

Tururu gaped. How could he be so bold? He glanced at his grandmother, expecting to see her lift her finger and blast him through the wall. Instead, she simply leveled a hard gaze at him.

Karari cleared his throat. "Anesu has no right to keep from me from what is mine. I've earned it."

"You've earned nothing yet."

The muscles in Karari's jaw tightened. He jabbed an accusing finger at Tururu. "You gave *him* an amulet. A stupid beginner. For six years I have done what you tell me. I have learned everything there is to learn."

Tururu shrank back when he saw the venom in Karari's eyes. Some kind of dark cloud was forming around him.

"You are not him." Grandmother was acting wary of Karari. She must be seeing the darkness too. "You were not chosen by Amai Vedu like Tururu—"

"*I* am the chosen one. It is my time. Your old-woman magic did not stop the Federation. My plan will at least show the whites that we will not take this lying down."

"Killing only brings more killing."

"The killing is here already. And it is our people who are dying."

"It is not Amai Vedu's way."

"It is not *your* way. It is time for change, and I am the one to lead the way. The people will follow me. Praise me. Remember me."

"You care nothing for our people. You only want power for yourself."

"Your time is over!" Karari kicked Grandmother's pouch across the floor. Tururu rushed to retrieve it.

"Leave it!" Karari cried. "Leave her. Come with me, and you will taste the life we are meant to live as rulers. I will teach you what you need to know."

Tururu turned to his grandmother. Why didn't she just teach him a lesson with her magic?

"Karari!" Grandmother said sharply.

He turned to face her, challenge in his eyes.

"Do not be lured by dark magic," she said, speaking very carefully, the way she did to him when he was about to make a mistake in a spell. "Do not let pride or lust for power lead you down a path from which there is no return. You will regret it."

He snorted and turned.

Her hand shot out and she grabbed him by the ear as she would an unruly child. She yanked him toward the door. "You need to be taught a lesson."

He tried to wriggle free. "I am no longer a child. You cannot treat me this way."

But she was bigger than he was and had a grip of steel. Twisting his ear, she led him outside, next to the eternal fire burning in the half-moon clearing in front of the hut. Karari stumbled along beside her, his face contorted with pain. Tururu followed, afraid of what might come but unable to not watch. The last time Grandmother had done something like this was shortly after she took Karari on as an apprentice. Thrusting Karari toward the well beside the hut, Grandmother pointed to a basin lying nearby.

"Fill that with water and bring it back here."

Finding his feet, Karari glared at her. "What for?"

"To get another chance. To learn humility. To learn what it truly means to be *godobori*."

Conflicted feelings played across Karari's face. The dark cloud around him began to lift but then hovered above him, rising and falling with each breath he took. Then he strolled toward the well, pretending to be unconcerned. Grandmother watched him. And Tururu understood why she didn't attack earlier. She seemed to be willing him to combat the darkness following him.

Smirking, Karari lowered the bucket into the well, filled the basin, then returned to stand in front of her. Water slopped over the edges of the bowl.

"Tururu!" she called, even though he was right behind her. Her eyes were pinned on Karari. "Bring the ceremony stool."

Tururu ran into the hut. What was Grandmother about to do? He hoped it didn't involve him in any way. He found the stool, an intricately carved piece of teak that reached his midsection. Grunting under its weight, he staggered outside and set it in front of Grandmother, then stepped back.

"Sit," she said.

Tururu turned toward Karari.

"You, Tururu," she said.

So he was to be part of this . . . whatever it was. Tururu backed away.

Grandmother glared at him.

With his insides doing flip-flops, he stood on tiptoe and slowly slid his bottom onto the stool. He hunched forward, trying to make himself as small as possible.

Grandmother pointed an imposing finger at Karari. "Wash Tururu's feet."

Tururu shrank down even farther. Karari gaped at her. And then with a cry of rage, he swung the basin around and hurled it at Tururu, hitting him in the head.

Tururu toppled sideways off the stool. Before he hit the ground, he was already thinking about scrambling to his feet. He had to get out of the way. Any minute now, Grandmother would be sending Karari to the ancestors.

But Grandmother just stood there, looking at Karari. Chest heaving, he glared back, the darkness settling over him like a blanket.

From the corner of his eye, Tururu saw the flames in the eternal fire swell, heard the familiar whispering and hissing of the *ngozi*. They were responding to Karari's fury, drawn to it. Grandmother's eyes flickered, but she kept them on Karari. It was almost as if she didn't notice the disturbance in the *ngozi*.

Karari turned slowly to stare wide-eyed at the mounting blaze. He took a step forward. Small, blue-tipped flames danced up toward him, murmuring as they did. Like a sleepwalker, he lifted his arm.

The *ngozi* rose in a quivering, luminous column and hung in front of him.

He gazed at it like a small child seeing fire for the first time and swayed from side to side. The fiery stream crackled and swayed in rhythm with him. He closed his eyes. His body tensed, tight as a hide drum, vibrating with some kind of power that made it look as if he might explode. The darkness around him swelled and expanded until it rose into the air like black smoke from an oil-infused fire. The *ngozi* hummed and grew in size, becoming as tall as Karari himself, taking his shape.

Grandmother lifted her arm. "No, Karari!"

Karari opened his eyes. They glowed with an eerie black light. Drawing his hand back, he jabbed his forefinger at her.

With a whoosh and a hiss, the *ngozi* streamed toward Grandmother's outstretched hand and enveloped it in a bright-blue blaze.

She shrieked and staggered back. Tururu charged toward her, trying to remember the magic word to douse fire. Still screeching, Grandmother clutched her forearm and spun this way and that. A chorus of jackals and wild dogs yipped and howled in response to her cry.

Tururu chased her around, trying to remember the magic word.

Grandmother collapsed onto her knees, clutching her forearm.

"G-g . . . *gasana!*" Tururu cried. "That's it!" He yelled the magic word over and over again, doubling over with the effort.

Grandmother continued to shriek.

Water.

His shirt was wet from water that had splashed out of the basin. Still shouting the magic word, he ripped it off and threw it over Grandmother's hand.

She screamed even louder and flung it off.

Flapping his hands at his mistake, he tried to think of what else he could do.

A blue light sparked over Grandmother's hand. With what seemed like superhuman effort, she lifted her head and closed her eyes. The only thing that moved were her lips, in a gasped incantation. The blue light over her hand dimmed and then, like molten gold, the *ngozi* poured back into the fire pit with a hiss.

Karari stood on the other side of the fire, the darkness gone from around him, his eyes no longer glowing with that dark, eerie light. He looked as shocked and frightened as Tururu.

He began moving toward her. "I—"

"Do not speak!" Still clasping her forearm, she struggled to her feet. Her body shook with the effort. She lifted pain-filled eyes to his.

"I curse you!" Her chest heaved with the effort it took to speak. "You will never know another moment's peace. Your soul will burn forever in the other world as my hand does now in this one. The ancestors curse you. The Goddess Gurutu will send her creatures to plague you." She swayed back and forth. "From this day on, you are no longer a disciple of Amai Vedu Africa, nor my apprentice. You are done."

"But I-I didn't mean . . ." Karari dropped to his knees, his face twisted with remorse. "Please. Forgive me."

Grandmother straightened with effort. Her words were slow and halting. "You made your choice. Go from this place."

Karari slowly rose to his feet and stared at her. He seemed uncertain but then, as if prompted from something inside, he took a deep breath. His expression hardened.

"I will go. But only because I no longer need you. Nothing will happen to me, because I am young and strong. Not old and weak like you."

The fire rose again. Within moments, it had increased tenfold. Karari glanced from the fire to Grandmother and then back again. Uncertainty played across his face. Tiny blue figures burst up and out like spray from a fountain in a strong wind, landing every which way outside the fire pit.

Tururu jumped back. He'd never seen anything like this happen before. The *ngozi* were out of control. "Grandmother!"

But she didn't seem to hear him. She just stood there like a rag doll, panting, as if it was taking everything to stay upright. He grabbed her good arm. She swayed toward him, eyes glazed with pain.

Tururu jabbed his finger toward the fire. "*Ngozi!*"

Grandmother jerked upright. "Amai Vedu!"

Keeping an eye on the flames, she pleaded with the Mother to give her strength. And then she stopped, as if hearing some private sound. She uttered a series of invocations. The *ngozi* hung in the air for a moment. Then, crackling and spitting embers, they shrank back down again.

Chest heaving, Grandmother took a shaky breath and sank to her knees.

Tururu ran to her side.

Karari stood on the other side of the fire, watching her. He didn't seem to know whether to go or stay. He looked down at his hands. "*Godobori*, I . . . please."

If Grandmother heard him, she gave no indication. Instead she held her forearm. And then, as if losing some inner battle, she lifted her gaze and stared at Karari with undisguised hatred. This time instead of calling on Amai Vedu, she screeched at him like an injured animal.

"Get away from me!" she cried. "I promise you this, you will suffer. Mark my words, the *ngozi* will soon claim you. You wait and see."

For a moment Karari looked like he might crumple to his knees, but then a shadow flitted across his face and he straightened. Planting his feet, he stood firm, fists clenched at his sides. He glanced down at the fire and then looked up at Grandmother, his mouth twisted in a sneer.

"*You* are the one who is suffering. You are the one the *ngozi* will claim. I have wasted enough time. We will meet again." He spun on his heel and headed for the open veld.

Grandmother seemed to deflate. "Oh, Amai Vedu," she whispered. "I have failed. Protect all of us in the times that are to come." She turned to Tururu. "Come. Help me to my hut."

Shooting a glance at Karari's retreating back, Tururu hefted her up and guided her toward her hut. She was drenched with sweat. He could feel the heat from her hand. It glowed with an eerie blue light. He blew on the charred, crippled mass.

"Thank you, Sabata," she said, "but save your breath. This pain is not only in my hand, but also deep inside my bones. And in my heart."

Sabata. He almost stopped dead in his tracks. She'd used his sacred Shona name. Chosen one. That could only mean one thing.

As if sensing his thoughts, she glanced at him, biting her lip against spasms of pain that made her shudder. "Yes, Sabata, you are to be the next *godobori.*"

He stopped and twisted around. "B-but, I am Tururu!"

"It is your destiny, my son. Now, help Grandmother inside."

Chapter 3

ELIZABETH FOLLOWED HER FATHER OUT TO THE FORD, slid onto the front seat, and slammed the door behind her. "So why's Mom want me to go with you to Mrs. B.'s? It's so boring there."

"It's 'Mrs. Bradley.' Don't be disrespectful." He started the car and then sat staring through the windshield.

"Will Andre and them be there?"

The three Bradley boys. The bane of her life. She'd so wanted to be friends with them in the beginning, especially Clive, the youngest, who taught her to bite her nails that first day. But then he started teasing and threatening her like the other two. Everything was a target for them. She always made sure Pookie was safely back in the coop when they came around. She'd seen how they'd teased their poor dog, now long missing. The time fifteen-year-old Andre teased her about her mother's pregnancy before Elizabeth even knew about it. Using words like "knocked up" and "preggers," he'd elbowed his two brothers like he'd just told a really funny joke. When Elizabeth's face blazed crimson with a combination of embarrassment and surprise, he laughed and made rude sounds. She should've kicked him in the shin, but she just wanted to cry.

"They went to Gwelo with Mr. Bradley." Her father backed down the driveway and swerved onto the washboard dirt road that led to the Bradley house.

"Good."

"You must tell me if they ever get funny with you. The Bradleys aren't going to do anything about them—boys will boys and it's only the *kaffirs* they're bothering and all that—but I will. I promise you that."

"I'm not afraid of them."

"That's good. But you just tell your old dad if they ever do anything you don't like, you hear me?"

She nodded and leaned her head against his shoulder. They bumped along the narrow road in a cloud of red dust. The sun perched over the water tower where the road joined the main highway to Gwelo.

Twenty minutes earlier, her father had hurried in from work, dressed in his good white shirt and smart khaki trousers, about to leave to drive Mrs. Emily Bradley to the train station. Then Elizabeth's mother asked him to take Elizabeth along. This was done in that stiff, not-really-talking tone her parents usually used after an argument. Jaw tight, he had gazed at his wife for a moment. Then, turning on his heel, gestured for Elizabeth to follow him. Luckily she looked presentable, her clothes clean, her hair still tightly plaited.

Even though she didn't like Mrs. Bradley, Elizabeth was pleased to be going along. It was always fun being with her dad. And maybe this time she'd actually see inside the Bradley house. She'd only been to the back door a couple of times when her dad had business with Mr. Bradley.

Mrs. Bradley was going to Salisbury to visit friends and to shop. More than half a day's journey away, Salisbury had everything big cities had to offer: garages selling the latest motor cars, blocks of shops filled with fashion. And then there was the big, swank, five-story Meikles Hotel with its elegant lounge. This time, Mrs. Bradley was off to a party at the Salisbury Cricket Club to celebrate Federation with friends. Mr. Bradley didn't go to such things. His trips were usually just to Gwelo, a small town seventy miles away with a large general store where he bought supplies every three months for the five families who lived in the thirty square miles of the valley. He wasn't one for fancy parties. He preferred the celebration the McKenzies held on supply day.

Elizabeth sneaked a glance at her father. He didn't seem as irritated about having to drive Mrs. Bradley as he usually was. He said she gave herself airs.

In the distance, lightning split the sky. A rainstorm. Oh, no, she shouldn't have soaked the ground; her sweet pea seeds would be drowned.

"When will we be back home?" she said.

He didn't answer. He appeared lost in thought.

She lifted her head from his shoulder and nudged him. "What's wrong?"

He gave a start. "Sorry. Daddy was just thinking about a little problem at work. Nothing you need worry about."

"Karari?"

He gave her a sharp look, then realization dawned on his face. "Aah, little pitchers have big ears."

"Honestly! Why do you always have to say that?"

"You've been eavesdropping again, haven't you?"

"I can't help it if people say things out loud sometimes and I sometimes hear them. Besides, Turu told me Karari's been chosen to be a big witch doctor."

"Well, at least he'll have one job."

"What happened?"

"I sacked him. He went and did it this time, trying to stir things up again. He's just making needless trouble for everybody."

"Are they going to riot like they did in Nyanga?"

"Where on earth did you get that from?"

"Mr. Osborne and Mom were talking about it when he delivered the dry ice."

"You don't eavesdrop, eh?"

"They were talking really loud, Dad."

"Uh huh. Anyway, for one thing, Nyanga's on the other side of the country. And for another that was hardly a riot, just a handful of drunken *kaffirs* getting stroppy. The problem is the bloody fools just don't understand Federation's for their own good. There are laws in place to protect their interests. But like the children they are, they expect to jump right into government and start running the country. But enough about that. No more eavesdropping and no more questions about all that nonsense. Just understand that Daddy would never let anything happen to his pearl of great price, do you hear me?"

He slid his arm over her shoulders and drew her close. She snuggled back against him.

The familiar rock outcropping and blue gum trees in front of the Bradley house slid into view. She wished her family had a nice, big place like that. Perhaps then her mother wouldn't always harp on her father about returning to South Africa. But Grandpa hadn't been in the right place at the right time like Mr. Bradley's father had back in the Thirties, when the government gave him and a group of other white settlers a bunch of land.

Her tutor, Mr. Coetzee, said the land was better off in the hands of the whites. They were smarter than the *kaffirs*. They could do more with it. Mr. Coetzee also said that if the Southern Rhodesian government hadn't taken the land some other government would have, and then the *kaffirs* would have been a lot worse off.

Her father swung into the Bradleys' driveway—two brick lanes split by a column of neatly mowed grass—and followed it around to the front of a thatched, rambling, brick house. Red hot poker blooms spiked up from a flower bed to the right of the house, while canna lilies, dahlias, daisies, gladioli, and other brightly colored flowers spilled out of flower beds running along a neatly trimmed, eight-foot-high hibiscus hedge.

They pulled up beside the front door. Squinting in the rearview mirror, her father ran his fingers through his wavy auburn hair and smoothed his moustache toward the corners of his mouth with thumb and forefinger.

"Be back in a jiffy." He headed for the front door. Wiping his feet on the sisal mat, he knocked, considered his feet, and then knocked again. A couple of moments later, a small, bullet-headed black man opened the door. The contrast between his black skin and his spotless white uniform was startling.

"Medem says to come in."

"Tell Madam I'll wait. Thank you, Chipo."

"Yes, bwana." He seemed uncertain for a moment whether or not to close the door, but then, leaving it open, retreated into the house.

Her father turned and winked at Elizabeth.

"Why don't you come in?" A smiling Mrs. Bradley appeared in the doorway clad in a pink dressing gown loosely belted at the waist. She held a glass of Scotch in each hand, one half-empty. Shoving the full glass into Mac's hand, she took a sip from the other and peered up at him, blue eyes sparkling.

"I-I thought I was late." Her father stared down at the drink for a moment, then gestured over his shoulder. "Uh, besides, I've got Elizabeth in the car."

The sparkle in Mrs. Bradley's eyes disappeared. Dabbing at her top lip with her pinkie, she tugged her dressing gown closed with one hand and frowned in Elizabeth's direction.

Elizabeth shrank down against the seat, feeling as if she'd somehow made a mistake in coming even though it wasn't her doing.

"Annie wasn't feeling well," her father continued. "I hope you don't mind."

"Well, I suppose it couldn't be helped." Mrs. Bradley's smile snapped back in place. She raised her glass and clinked it against her father's. "Cheers!"

He hesitated and glanced back at Elizabeth. She gave him a questioning look. He looked away.

"Come, now! If you're not going to be civilized and come in, the least you can do is toast Federation with me."

He took a sip and gasped. "Whoa!"

"Oh, honestly. I've seen you down your share of doubles before."

He shuddered. "Not this early in the morning."

Elizabeth straightened in her seat, feeling the urge to tell Mrs. Bradley to stop pestering her father to drink her stupid drink.

"And here I thought you were a spur-of-the-moment sort of bloke."

"Sometimes."

"That's the spirit!" She clinked his glass again and downed the rest of her drink.

Her father hesitated, then emptied his glass. He shuddered again, and she laughed. Taking the glass from him, she spun on her heel and headed back into the house. "Be back in a moment."

Wiping his mouth with the back of his hand, her father glanced back at Elizabeth.

"That'll be the day," he mouthed.

She managed a grin. What had changed to make Mrs. Bradley so friendly all of a sudden? She never used to be.

Her father lit a cigarette and paced up and down the front step while he smoked, glancing at his watch every now and then until Chipo appeared, lugging a trunk and hatbox. Her father helped him load them into the back of the car. Mrs. Bradley finally appeared wearing white gloves, a black-and-white halter-neck dress, and her usual backless shoes that sounded like a machine gun on the cement floor.

Her father opened the passenger-side door and inclined his head toward the back. "Come on now, Elizabeth, hop over. There's a good girl."

Elizabeth took her time clambering over the seat, aware that Mrs. Bradley was glaring at her. She finally made it over and fell back against the backseat, as if exhausted. Her father frowned at her.

Mrs. Bradley slid in and her father closed the door. "Elizabeth, where are your manners? Say hello to Mrs. Bradley."

"Hello, Mrs. Bradley."

"Hello, Elizabeth," Mrs. Bradley said without turning around. That's the one thing Elizabeth appreciated about her—she never pretended to like children, not even her own.

Her father got in and started the car. Shifting across the seat until she was inches from him, Mrs. Bradley pulled the rearview mirror toward her and angled it in. "I've got something in my eye."

"Do you want to go back into the house?" her father asked.

She probed for a moment more. "Got it!" Dabbing at the corner of her eye with a handkerchief, she settled back against the seat.

Elizabeth frowned. That was where her mother usually sat.

Her father repositioned the rearview mirror and, with an uneasy glance at Mrs. Bradley, he reversed down the driveway. They headed toward the train station. Elizabeth glared at the back of Mrs. Bradley's head and tried to catch her father's eye in the rearview mirror, to share a joke at Mrs. Bradley's expense. He stared straight ahead.

"Lloyd was quite impressed with that little tactic of yours," Mrs. Bradley said, laying her head back against the seat. "Making that *kaffir*, what's-his-name, the boss boy. That was a clever move."

"Mfuni. Actually it wasn't a tactic. He's a damned good worker—or should I say, *was*. He's missing. That's why I was late. I hope something hasn't happened to him. I'm afraid the promotion could make the troublemakers, Karari especially, target him."

"Cigarette?"

"Please."

Mrs. Bradley removed two cigarettes from her silver case and stuck them both in her mouth. Her father reached into his pocket for his lighter and handed it to her. Mrs. Bradley lit the cigarettes and handed him one.

Blowing smoke, she stared down at the lighter. "This is rather nice."

He took the cigarette. "I thought I'd lost it."

She flipped it over and began to read. "To my dearest husband, with all my love, your lady Annabel." She handed it back to him. "Impressive."

Elizabeth glared at Mrs. Bradley's profile. She didn't look impressed.

"A wedding present." Her father slipped the lighter back into his pocket and took a drag on his cigarette.

Mrs. Bradley leaned playfully against him. "She's a very lucky woman."

"I'm a very lucky man."

Elizabeth slid forward and, resting her chin on her forearms, stuck her nose between the two of them. And that's where she stayed until they reached the train station.

Chapter 4

TURURU WATCHED HIS GRANDMOTHER THRASH ABOUT on her mattress, her face twisted in pain. The sweet, cloying scent of burned flesh hung over her like a shroud.

He didn't know what else he could do. He'd just applied a second poultice to her injured hand—a slimy gray concoction that made him retch. Had he got it right this time? In a moment of clarity, she'd told him about the dried coddia leaves he needed to add for *ngozi* burns. After a desperate search among her many jars of herbs and powders, he'd finally found what looked to be the right one and quickly mixed a new batch.

Sinking down beside her, Tururu willed the *muti* to work. She looked so helpless without her *douk*. He'd never seen her bare head before. Was she going to die?

Grandmother stopped tossing and her face relaxed into a peaceful sleep. The poultice was working.

Tururu gave a sigh and sat back on his heels. He glanced through the hut's arched doorway into the blinding midmorning glare outside. Flies buzzed around the doorway, kept away by one of Grandmother's spells.

He thought about what Grandmother had said earlier, how she'd wanted to set the *ngozi* on Karari to destroy him. When Tururu asked why she hadn't, she told him she'd sworn an oath to Amai Vedu to work for the good of all her people, even Karari. She also told him that Karari had come into his own too early, growing more powerful than she had realized. And now he had aroused the *ngozi* before he knew how to control them. He could use their power for what he wanted, but they would slowly take him over. In the end, they would consume him in their fight to become human.

Despite himself, Tururu missed Karari. Even though the twenty-year-old and his big plans of getting back at the whites had come between him and his friend Mfuni, Karari had been a hero to him, an elder brother. Sometimes he even helped Tururu with his own potions. And now Karari was gone and Mfuni was gone, and he, Tururu, was to be *godobori*.

It was all too much.

But he must be brave. Grandmother said that when Amai Vedu saved him that hot October day two years earlier, it was not so he could be *n'anga*, as she had thought. It was because he was to be *godobori*.

Tururu remembered. It had been peanut-harvesting time. He was alone, checking the field behind the Bradley house for leftover peanuts, like he did after every harvest. Pickings were usually slim—what the workers didn't find, the birds did. He had just unearthed a nice big, fat peanut when, out the corner of his eye, he saw the three Bradley brothers heading toward him across the field.

He shoved the peanut into his pocket and slid a glance toward the water tower and the open veld. He could make a run for it, but they'd catch him for sure and he'd probably get a beating. Over the years, other than getting pelted with rocks a couple of times, he'd managed to stay out of their way. All he could do was hope that they would soon tire of making sport of him.

But he had a sinking feeling this time would be different. He could tell by bwana Andre's purposeful stride and the way bwana Clive kept his head down. Bwana Ian trailed behind them, letting loose with his slingshot every few minutes. Rocks whizzed close to his head, making soft thuds in the dirt around him.

Tururu ignored the rocks and silently begged Amai Vedu to protect him. As the boys drew closer, Tururu could see that Clive carried an enamel bowl in his hands. He seemed to be hanging back. Andre prodded him forward.

"Hey, *kaffir!*" Andre called.

Tururu turned, pretending to be surprised. "Bwana?"

When the boys were just a few feet away, Clive suddenly veered to the right. Andre grabbed him by his shirt and shoved him toward Tururu. Clive usually went along with Andre, the leader of the three. If *he* was afraid of what was happening, it must be bad.

"We've got some *lekker sadza* for you." Grinning, Andre shoved Clive's reluctant hands with the bowl under Tururu's nose.

Crispy bits of pork crackling floated enticingly in a pool of grease atop a small mountain of cooked cornmeal. Tururu stared at the *sadza* and took a step back. What was in there? Dog shit? Bwana shit? Bits of glass?

Andre grabbed the bowl from Clive and jammed it into Tururu's chest. Grease slopped onto the front of his shirt. "Eat it. All of it. Now!"

Tururu knew as soon as he took his first mouthful that something was wrong. There was a bitter taste that made the back of his tongue tingle. He worked his jaw, holding the *sadza* in his mouth. He eyed the open veld.

Andre grabbed him by the back of the neck in a vicious grip. "Swallow, *kaffir!* That's perfectly good *sadza*, you ungrateful sod. You're going to finish every last bit, hey? Or I will sit on your chest and stuff it all down your bleddy throat and you will choke and vomit and make a big bleddy mess all over yourself. Do you want that, hey?"

Calling on Amai Vedu again, he swallowed.

"There's a good *kaffir*," Andre said. "Now finish it."

Tururu dutifully shoveled down the *sadza*, grease dripping down his chin. Ian drew closer, looking eager, a hyena slinking in for a kill. Clive looked away.

Bwana Bradley's voice boomed from the edge of the field. "Hey, you lot! Get your arses back here, right now!"

"Coming!" Andre snatched the almost-empty bowl from Tururu's hands. "Sorry *kaffir*, we've got to run. We'll see you around. Or not." Ian giggled and the three of them took off, Clive leading the pack. Laughing, Andre and Ian threw glances back at Tururu as they ran toward the house.

Tururu was halfway across the peanut field when the pain in his stomach began. Clutching himself, he doubled over. Without warning, his bowels opened and he let loose a stream of diarrhea. In the distance, he could hear the boys hooting and cackling. Maybe he could make it to the water tower, where he could wash himself under the tap.

But then the pain grew worse as if Andre had Tururu's stomach gripped in his fist and was twisting it into a tight ball. He had to get to Grandmother's hut. Ignoring his soiled shorts, he stumbled across the uneven field. But before he could go any farther, his body convulsed, the world spun, and he fell facedown in the dirt. The cloying, rootlike odor of peanut and fresh soil filled his nostrils.

He curled up into a ball of agony. The world disappeared from view, and all he could hear was his heart thumping in his ears like a ceremonial drum.

And then, as if in a dream, he could see himself emerging from his mother's womb as she squatted on the veld to give birth to him behind a bush. Time shifted, and in quick succession he was trying to find Grandmother's invisible hut. From far off he could hear a voice talking to him. He strained to hear.

"It is time, Sabata! You must hurry or you will die."

The images faded, but something arose within him—a power he'd never felt before. He knew what he had to do. His spirit rose from his body, weightless and free. He looked down at his motionless form below, eyelids pinched shut. He sensed Amai Vedu's spirits willing him on. Reaching down into his body, he scooped out what appeared to be a small mass of red pinpricks and flung them skyward. He watched them flicker in the air, then disappear.

What seemed ages later, he was sucked back into his body, gasping for air. It felt as if a rasp was being forced through the entire length of his intestines, yanking them inside out. There was a metallic taste in his mouth. He struggled to his knees and vomited in great gasping spasms until it felt as if the sides of his stomach were rubbing against each other.

Wiping his mouth with the back of his hand, he struggled to his feet. In fits and starts, he staggered toward the water tower and the tap beneath it. He drank until he thought his stomach would burst. He lay there for as long as he dared, then lurched toward the safety of his grandmother's hut.

One glance was all it took. She knew what had happened and quickly mixed him a potion. She told him later that he'd been fed a large dose of what the whites called "opening medicine," which caused the diarrhea. But there had also been a small dose of *ubuthi* added, some kind of poison she didn't recognize.

"You passed Amai Vedu's test." She tied a pouch around his neck containing the most essential of her special powders, along with a sacred amulet she had prepared for him. Each time he used his magic, part of it would stay in his amulet and add to its power. Its power would grow with his.

Now a weak voice murmured, "Sabata."

He kneeled beside her. "What is it, Grandmother?"

"I will be all right now. You must go."

"But—"

"Go, I tell you. I do not want to give your father any excuse to keep you away. Besides, Grandmother must sleep."

He rose slowly and turned to go.

"Sabata," she said in a stronger voice. "Do not worry. You will be a worthy successor."

Tururu wanted to believe her, but he still had so much to learn.

Chapter 5

ELIZABETH SLIPPED HER HAND INTO HER FATHER'S AS they stood watching the passenger train chug away from the single-platform station. Mrs. Bradley was the only one to board, joining passengers from Northern Rhodesia and other parts of Southern Rhodesia, most of them headed for the beaches of South Africa. Two days earlier, her father had been down at the station with his workers loading sisal onto a cargo train bound for processing in South Africa, where it would be turned into rope.

"Well, that's that then, hey?" her father said, turning to go.

She grinned up at him. "Race you to the car."

As if galvanized by a starter's pistol, they both started running toward the Ford parked in the shade thirty yards away on the other side of the long, corrugated storage building. A mass of dark clouds had gathered overhead. She reached the car first.

"You don't have to let me win, you know," she said, not meaning it.

Bending over to catch his breath, he glanced up and grinned. "It's the least a father can do."

"Honestly?"

He glanced around as if somebody might hear what he was about to say. "I gave it my all."

Pleased at this admission, she piled into the car beside him. There was a growl of thunder, and the heavens opened. Her father started the car and switched on the windshield wipers.

"Oh no," she said. "My poor sweet pea seeds."

"Oh, they'll be all right. It's probably not even raining at home."

"Hurry, all right?"

He glanced at his watch. "Oh, you'd better believe it."

They drove in a comfortable silence through the pounding rain for a few minutes. And then the storm was over.

"Dad, did you ever wish I'd been a boy?"

He gave her a sharp look. "Never. Why?"

"Well, I've heard Mom tell people she always wanted a boy."

"Well, that's just because she has a girl. Now she wants a matched set."

She nodded, but she knew better.

Reaching over, he gave her a one-armed squeeze and a quick kiss on the side of her head before turning into their driveway. He hurried toward the house while Elizabeth headed for her sweet pea bed. The crackling strains of the BBC announcer on the radio drifted from the house: "the thirty-three-year-old New Zealander, along with his companion, Tenzing Norgay, were honored today at the Adventurers Club in London for their conquest of Mount Everest. In other news, after the signing of the Federation of Rhodesia and Nyasaland, those present had this to say: The Federation of Rhodesia and Nyasaland will be good for all concerned. The few dissenters in London and Central Africa are troublemakers who do not represent the views of the vast majority. Most black Africans clearly recognize the benefits of closer association, indeed the Federation . . ." Static drowned out the rest. Elizabeth reached the flower bed. Her father was right—it had hardly rained there.

Before the big rains came, she would have to cover the sweet peas with the mahohoboho tree's spadelike leaves—the ones she used to use in the old days to cover her fairy village. She glanced toward the servant's quarters, hoping Turu had returned early from his grandmother's. But there was no sign of him.

Her stomach growled. Teatime. When they'd left, her mother had been telling Nelson to make scones. She skipped to the house and up the steps.

"With liquor on your breath!"

Elizabeth froze. Her mother's raised voice was coming from the bedroom.

"I had one drink, for God's sake. You know how it is. I was just being polite."

"Yes, I know how it is, all right. Just like you were being polite at the party a couple of Sundays ago."

"I told you. *She* kissed *me*. You know how she gets after a couple of drinks. I couldn't help it—"

"Is that when she asked you to drive her to the station?"

"What do you mean?"

"So she *was* the one who asked you, then?"

"I told you. I do what Bradley tells me to do. I can't be rude to her. She's the boss's wife, for God's sake."

The snap of a lighter, and then her mother said very quietly, "You don't want this baby, do you?"

"What?"

"Admit it. It's one more thing to tie you down."

"Tie me down?" he cried. "Do you think I left university and a good, safe, paying job in Northern Rhodesia because I wanted to be *free*? Do you think I lived with your bloody parents for two years because I wanted to be *free*? Oh, honestly Annie, you're being ridiculous. And unfair. Of course I want this baby, just as much as you do. But frankly I'm worried about you after all you went through with Elizabeth. You're the most important person in the world to me—"

"Oh, spare me."

A door slammed, and there was silence.

Elizabeth plopped into a chair. She hated when her parents fought. Why was her mother so unreasonable? She was always in a bad mood or crying. The worst of it all, though, was that Elizabeth's name always came up when they spoke about the coming baby, like she'd been bad.

Her father entered the kitchen, lighting a cigarette. He took a drag, and, blowing out smoke, stared down at the inscription on his lighter before dropping it into his shirt pocket. He glanced up and saw Elizabeth. His face brightened.

"There's my girl! How are the sweet peas coming along?"

Suddenly she was angry with him. "I just planted them."

"You were worried about them drowning."

She shrugged. "They're all right."

He leaned back against the sideboard and gave her a fond look. "Remember how you were always worrying about that fairy village of yours?"

"Good grief, Dad, that was ages ago when I was a little child."

He grinned. "I liked the idea that we were supporting fairies."

"I'm too old for that."

"You're never too old to believe in magic. I still do, you know."

She rolled her eyes.

"I do, really. Magic happens when you believe with all your heart and mind, and trust that something is possible. It takes imagination. And courage." He gave her a crooked grin. "You've got all that, my little pearl of great price. Your fairies were magnificent."

He walked over and kissed her on the forehead. "I've got to head back to work, see you in a couple of hours."

<hr />

After tea Elizabeth headed for her bedroom, where she lay on her back on the cool cement floor. The tin roof creaked as the sun beat down on it. In minutes, she was asleep. She was awoken by the murmurs of her parents' voices coming from the lounge. She stared up at the ceiling. Not another argument, please. She listened. No, they were talking normally. Yawning and stretching, she rose and headed for them. She peeked around the door. Her mother sat on her husband's lap, his arm around her. Giving a sigh of relief, Elizabeth strode into the room.

"There's my girl," her father said. "Finish your homework?"

"Uh huh."

"Hungry? Want something to eat?"

"No, thank you. I had a couple of scones and jam."

"Come, sit by us."

Elizabeth perched on the arm of the chair.

"Whose girl are you?" he asked, hugging her close.

"Daddy's," she said, in the usual little game they played. "Can I have sixpence to go and buy some sweets?"

He shifted around in order to reach into his pocket.

"*May* I," her mother said. "And no, you may not. You haven't had your lunch yet."

"I ate already. I just told you."

"That wasn't a proper lunch. Anyway, I don't want you wandering all over creation by yourself. Right now van Zyl's shop is too far away for my liking."

"Turu'll go with me." Elizabeth nudged her father. "We'll come right back, I promise."

"Oh, certainly," her mother said. "I'm just going to let you go off across kingdom come alone with a *kaffir* with all the trouble we're having."

"He's *Turu*," Elizabeth said. "He's my friend."

"He is *not* your friend, and don't let me ever hear you saying that in public, do you hear me?"

"He's a good boy. You said so yourself."

"I said no such thing."

"You did too."

"Don't be cheeky with me. Anyway, he's getting too old for you to be playing with him anymore." She turned to her father. "I thought you were going to be using him more in the fields."

"It's Saturday. He works for me two days a week. That's enough for now. Come on, let them go. What fun does she have but the occasional sweet down at van Zyl's?" He reached into his pocket for the money.

"We'll be back in a jiffy. You'll see, Mom" Elizabeth said, adding to her father, "Turu too?"

Taking out a half a crown and a shilling, he handed them to Elizabeth. "There you are."

Elizabeth stood. "Thanks!"

Hoisting herself up with one hand on the arm of the chair, the other hand on her stomach, her mother got to her feet. "Do what you like. I don't care."

"Annie, please stay," her father said.

She eased back down onto his lap.

"Well, I'd better be off, then," Elizabeth said, giving them each a quick peck on the cheek.

"You know, seeing as how you're going, you might as well get me a bottle of milk," her mother said. "Doc Goodwin says I should be drinking more fresh milk, instead of the powdered. Though it galls me to pay that crook's exorbitant prices."

Her father dug back in his pocket. "Think about the poor *kaffirs* who have to pay those prices all the time, unless they have good employers like us who give rations." He handed Elizabeth another half a crown.

Her mother frowned down at Elizabeth's feet. "Where are your shoes?"

"I can't find them," Elizabeth said automatically, heading for the door.

"You're asking for sandworms again."

"Yes, Mom."

"Shoes!" her mother cried as Elizabeth skipped down the hallway.

She almost tripped over Nelson, who was on all fours applying a thick, waxy swirl of red polish to the concrete floor: preparations for Sunday's *braaivleis*, when Mr. Bradley returned from Gwelo with the next few months' supplies.

"Is Turu back yet?"

Sitting back on his heels, Nelson glared at her.

"Come on Nelson, just tell me. You don't always have to act like that."

"No!" He jerked his head for her to get out of his way.

She sauntered toward the door.

Making tch-tch sounds, he continued smearing polish on the floor.

Skipping down the back steps, Elizabeth glanced toward the blue gum trees for signs of Turu. He was late. Elizabeth's old diapers, washed and bleached in preparation for the baby, flapped on the clothesline. She headed for her swing, hanging from a thick branch on the avocado tree. Halfway up its trunk, scraps of wood signaled the beginning of their fort. She slipped onto the swing, gave a shove, and pumped as hard as she could—until the ropes buckled.

Something white flashed at the bottom of the yard, and she stopped pumping. One of the chickens? No, they were either in the coop or on the other side of the garage where they liked to forage this time of day. Turu? She peered toward the blue gums. No sign of him. Besides, he didn't have any white clothes.

The back of her neck prickled. Who could it be? A marauding rebel from Nyanga? She started to pump her legs again, keeping them in the air every time the swing dropped back down, away from imaginary hands that might reach out from the earth to grab her. The screen door squealed and her father emerged from the house carrying a locked metal toolbox. Nelson followed with a broom and a bowl of cooked cornmeal.

Relief flooded her, for some reason. "Dad!"

"Hey, little girl."

He flashed her a grin and headed toward the fortified storeroom behind Nelson's quarters where the bulk goods for the five families in the valley were stored. Mr. van Zyl, a bachelor, didn't share in the arrangement, what with his business of selling to everyone else. Mr. Bradley's father had set up the system when he and his family lived in what was now Elizabeth and her family's house. That was before he built the Bradleys' current house.

"When you're finished, will you please come over here by me 'til Turu comes back?" she called.

Her father dropped the toolbox onto the scarred wooden table outside the larder, drowning out her words.

"Dad?"

But he had already unlocked the larder door, and he and Nelson disappeared into its depths. She could hear them shifting around the big tin drums holding flour, cornmeal, and sugar while Nelson swept and her father collected the saucers of cornmeal and strychnine he'd set out for the rats. A short while later, he emerged from the larder followed by Nelson, who had four dead rats dangling from his fist. Not looking where he was going, Nelson tripped over her father's heels. He stumbled and almost dropped the saucers he was carrying.

"Dammit, man. What the hell's the matter with you today?"

Mumbling apologies, Nelson glanced toward the bottom of the yard and then hurried toward the rubbish bin at the side of the garage. Her father unlocked the toolbox and removed a brown paper packet tied with string. Strychnine. He always kept it under lock and key, like it was the crown jewels or something. Placing it on the table, he headed back into the larder.

Elizabeth kept swinging, trying to touch the leaves with her toes. Trying to see what was down at the bottom of the yard. She felt safe now that her father was close by.

"What the hell?" her father cried.

At the top of an upswing, Elizabeth glanced down to see her father staring up at the sky. She turned in time to see a hawk eagle soaring into the air with something clutched in its claws. Struggling to slow the swing's momentum, she jumped off and ran toward her father. Nelson ran from the larder.

"What happened?" she cried.

Her father gave her a blank stare, then looked back up at the sky. "I don't believe it. That bloody bird just stole the poison."

"Maybe it thought the packet was something to eat."

"I wish I could've caught that on camera."

"Nelson!" her mother called from the house.

Staring openmouthed up at the sky, Nelson seemed to come to and hurried toward the house.

"Hey, Annie, come out here for a moment!" her father called. "You won't believe this."

"Can't, I'm right in the middle of something."

"I'd like a pet like that," Elizabeth said.

"Don't you go getting any ideas, my girl." Her father looked around, as if unsure what to do next. "No giving chase, you hear me?"

Elizabeth didn't answer, too busy wondering where the bird might have gone.

Turu appeared from the behind the blue gum trees.

Finally. "Where've you been?" she cried.

He shrugged and headed toward them.

"Listen," her father said, turning back to lock the larder. "I've got to get over to Doc Goodwin for your mother's pills, and then I'm going back to the sheds for a couple of hours. Remember what I told you, hey?"

Without waiting for an answer, he strode toward the house.

Elizabeth ran to Turu and held up the coins her dad had given her. "Guess what?"

"Fun Sails?"

"Van Zyl's, is that all you have to say?" She frowned. "What's the matter with you?"

"*Picannin dona!*" Nelson appeared from the house and waddled toward them, holding out a shilling. He seemed calmer than he had been earlier. "Sunlight soap."

"Say please."

"*Checha.*"

"Don't you dare tell me to hurry." Elizabeth snatched the coin from his fingers. "I'll come back when I'm good and ready."

He glared at her. "Medem say."

She nudged Turu and turned to go.

Nelson grabbed Turu's elbow. "You must stay."

"He *has* to go with me." Elizabeth took Turu's other arm. "My dad said so."

Nelson held on for a moment, glaring at Elizabeth, but then released Turu's elbow. Glancing around, he leaned close to Turu and said something Elizabeth couldn't quite understand. Something about the beer hall.

Turu stared at him, clearly alarmed.

"Come on, Turu," Elizabeth said, pulling him away. "Let's go."

Chapter 6

TURURU FOLLOWED ELIZABETH TOWARD THE BLUE GUM trees at the bottom of the yard, brooding. His father's warning to stay away from the beer hall had triggered the dark feeling that had been plaguing him since the night before. Was it a dream he couldn't remember? Or had this whole business with Karari just unnerved him? And what did father mean about "meddling"?

"Hey," Elizabeth said. "I'm talking to you."

He stopped. She had asked him something, and he had not even noticed it.

"What was that about the beer hall?"

He shrugged and kept walking, wishing she would be quiet for a moment so he could sort through this feeling of his.

"Come on, just tell me."

He shrugged again.

"You're in a funny old mood, aren't you?"

He nodded.

"I know what—let's drive your car over there."

Without waiting for an answer, she turned and headed toward the side of the garage where Tururu kept his toy wire car. This was a passion of his, fashioning scraps of wire—anything from coat hangers to lengths of de-barbed fence wire—into shoebox-size, skeletal shapes of cars. To "drive" the contraptions, he twisted two thick wires into a column that came to his waist, topped by a "steering wheel." He was also working on a motorbike he'd once seen in a picture. If he had his way, he'd make things out of wire all day long.

Tururu hurried after her. She always managed to twist his car out of shape to where it wouldn't roll properly, and then he had to spend hours readjusting it. Rushing past her, he removed the two lengths of corrugated tin covering his hiding space in a crevice between the chicken coop and the garage, and then carefully removed the car. It was shaped as much like the McKenzies' Ford as he could make it. Bwana had congratulated him on his skill and started saving bits of wire for him. Elizabeth stopped him as he was about to replace the two lengths of tin.

"Wait a minute. What's that?" She pointed at his latest creation at the back of the hiding place—a small, half-finished, bubble-roofed car.

"For *bebe*." He slipped the tin back into place and turned to go.

She gave him a friendly shove. "You never made *me* my own car."

He continued walking, guiding the car in front of him. "Missi not bwana."

"You just don't like how I drive. That's it, isn't it?"

He steered the car back toward the path without answering her. The wire wheels glided effortlessly over the ground.

"Can I drive?" she called.

He stopped and stepped to one side. "Please, missi, do not push down."

She took the steering wheel with both hands. "I know, I know." She inched the car over the uneven ground, stopping every few seconds to ease it over a rough spot. It took them an age to get to the opening between the blue gum trees. Tururu trailed behind, eyes narrowed.

"See?" she said turning to grin at him. "I'm getting the hang of—" She stamped her foot. Even from where Tururu stood, he knew what had happened. He sighed and went to check the damage.

"I was being very gentle. You saw that. Why's it do that to me? Every time."

Clucking his tongue, Tururu bent down and made a couple of adjustments to the wire frame. "All the time, Tururu show missi—"

"I did *not* push hard!" she cried. "You saw me. You saw how soft I pushed."

"Like so." He straightened, lightly grasped the steering wheel and, with two fingers, guided the car along.

"Oh, why don't you just drive? Otherwise we're never going to get there."

Tururu shrugged but felt relieved since he thought the same thing. He led the way, guiding the car past the last orderly row of sisal plants. The air vibrated with the thrum of crickets. They walked in a comfortable silence and turned onto the path toward van Zyl's shop.

Almost right away, it felt as if Jasu, God of the Sun, had turned his face toward them. The deep green of the sisal turned to hard, scrubby grass the color of a lion's haunch. The smell of rain hung in the air. On the distant horizon in front of them, the huge baobab tree beside bwana van Zyl's shop looked like a fat stalk with tiny twigs branching upward. Acacia and other thorn trees dotted the veld. Three hundred yards away, five eland buck appeared out of nowhere and floated on a heat wave past the jagged outline of his people's ruins.

Chapter 7

ELIZABETH STOPPED. "WHY DON'T YOU JUST TELL ME where Grandmother's hut is?"

"Tururu already tell—"

"I know, I know. It's invisible and magic and all that. Even so, I bet I know exactly where it is." She swung around, thought for a moment, and then jabbed a finger in the direction of a distant rise with a single black monkey thorn tree on top.

The spot where he called forth Grandmother's hut. How could she possibly know that?

She turned back to face him. "Well?"

"Phfft." He gave a dismissive shake of his head. He felt bad he couldn't tell her, but she was white, after all. And a nonbeliever. He began to jog. The car almost floated above the ground in front of him.

Elizabeth charged past him. She was always racing him, even when he wasn't racing. He let her take the lead.

A low rumble shook the ground, followed by a thunderous crash. Charcoal-tinged clouds appeared out of nowhere, blotting out the sun. Lightning blazed across the sky. Then, as if someone had overturned a massive bucket of water, rain poured down, soaking them. Elizabeth pulled her braid forward over the top of her head and slowed to a walk. A dark *V* traveled down her back.

Then, as quickly as it had disappeared, the sun was back. Golden shafts of light streamed through thick black clouds and sheets of rain.

"Monkey's wedding!" Blinking raindrops from her eyes, she threw back her head and opened her mouth.

"Why missi always say that?"

"Somewhere out there, a monkey's getting married. You see, they wait for the sun to shine through the rain and then they get married. Like when bwanas and misses get married in a church, with big white dresses and tuxedos and confetti and a lovely big white cake with marzipan and icing and flowers—and everything."

"Monkeys?"

She burst out laughing. "Oh, honestly, it's just a saying. But it *is* supposed to be a time of magic, you know, so you need to make a wish." She closed her eyes.

He stared at her. Was she was lying again? She did it so often and seemed to enjoy it so much.

She opened one eye. "Well? This is a special time. Don't waste it. Just close your eyes and make a wish. Something you want to happen—you know, like in my case, I wish something would happen around here, or I wish I would never have to go to boarding school. Or in your case, you could wish your dad wasn't so nasty, or something like that." She considered him through dripping lashes for a moment. "Well? What are you waiting for?"

"This bwana's magic?"

"No, it's not," she said. "It's just ordinary old magic for any old body . . . Oh, honestly, just make a bloody wish, will you? You're going to make me miss *my* wish. I swear!"

He pinched his eyes shut to stop her carrying on. The sound of rain pelting the ground sounded louder with his eyes closed. He tried to remember what had made him feel so uneasy.

He fingered his amulet. Maybe the bwana's magic would help Grandmother get better sooner. Did that count as a wish?

"There!" Elizabeth cried.

Tururu opened his eyes. She was staring at him.

"Did you make a wish?"

He shrugged.

"Oh, honestly. You never listen to me. Well, you missed your chance." With a flounce, she turned and started back down the path, splashing as she went.

They walked in silence while the rain streamed down. And then, as suddenly as it had started, it stopped. All that remained of the clouds were gray shreds drifting across the face of the sun. Two hundred yards ahead, van Zyl's shop appeared as if it had been hiding behind the sheets of rain.

The squat building with its uneven, homemade-brick walls and flat, corrugated roof rested in the narrow shade of the baobab tree—thirty feet of elephantine trunk topped with stubby, twisted rootlike branches. According to Shona legend, when the people made Amai Vedu Africa mad, she yanked out the biggest shade trees in Mashonaland and planted them all upside down to teach her people a lesson. Now the only shade the baobab provided came from the thick trunk, and only when it was at just the right angle to the sun.

Elizabeth trotted past Tururu. "Race you."

Again? Tururu charged forward, his car almost floating above the path in front of him. They ran together most of the way, until she burst out in front of him. He caught up to her at the steps leading into the shop. Puffing and panting, they both doubled over.

Catching his breath, Tururu straightened. "Tururu let missi win."

"You did not," she said between breaths. "I wasn't even running with all my might." She started up the steps, yanked open the screen door, and let it slam behind her.

"Don't slam the bleddy door, man," bwana van Zyl said. "Close. It. How many times have I got to tell you bleddy kids?"

Tururu's stomach clenched at the sound of the man's voice. He never knew what to expect from him. It could be anything from silently ignoring him to a beating. Taking his time, he parked his car between the shop and a clump of bushes, then started slowly up the steps.

The door flew open, almost knocking him over. Elizabeth frowned down at him. "Come on, don't dawdle."

Following her into the shop, he carefully shut the door behind him. The air was dense with the mixed odors of sulfur, cornmeal, tobacco, and the bwana's whiskey breath. Keeping his eyes down, he hurried across the dusty cement floor between sacks of flour, cornmeal, and sugar to catch up to Elizabeth. She could deflect some of the nonsense he was about to catch from the bwana.

To his right, a framed photograph of the bwanas' new queen smiled coolly down at him. Medem Queen Elizabeth's picture was in the newspaper last year when they put that big crown on her head. His eyes strayed to a yellowing, typewritten notice beneath the picture that had been sticky-taped to the wall. Thanks to *his* Elizabeth, who had been teaching him to read, he knew what most of the words meant.

It said that *muntu* must be kept out of White Parliament. Europeans were to support the Rhodesia Council in favor of Federation and they should be the artisans and typists and clerks. *Muntu* should be the ones to grow food and should be kept out of the towns, except those who had to come in to serve whites. At the bottom, it said: "Let the White Man Remember the White Man—Always."

Tururu knew this sign had a lot to do with Mfuni and some of the others in the valley joining Karari to plot against the bwanas. They were going to let the bwanas know they were not going to take the new Federation lying down. Tururu had listened in on these sessions at the back of the beer hall, flattered that they allowed him to stay even though he was so much younger.

At first Tururu was caught up in the excitement, the anger that Karari could whip up. But as the meetings went on, Tururu had become more and more uncomfortable. Especially when the talk turned to killing. He could see something changing in Karari, a darkness around him he couldn't explain. It reminded Tururu of the small cruelties he himself had suffered at Karari's hands, and how merciless Karari could be to anybody who challenged him. Grandmother said that killing only brought more killing. He'd stopped going. Nobody had challenged him because of Grandmother. But his friendship with Mfuni had suffered.

"Hey, *kaffir*, what the hell you looking at?" bwana van Zyl bellowed. "You can't read the bleddy sign, so just move on."

Tururu quickly slipped beside missi, who was peering into a glass case filled with penknives and rifles at the far end of the counter. She loved penknives. He risked a glance at the bwana. He was still glaring at Tururu. They couldn't dawdle too much longer.

Keeping one bloodshot eye on them, van Zyl turned and started stacking tins of corned beef onto the shelf behind him. His short-sleeved shirt strained across his belly. A cigarette smoldered over the edge of the long, wooden counter pockmarked with cigarette burns. "What's it to be?" he bellowed.

"Milk, please Mr. van Zyl," Elizabeth said. "And two bars of Sunlight soap, please."

She had used her extra-nice voice, the one she reserved for when she wanted something. That meant she was going to steal sherbit from the jar by the bwana's elbow, before or after using the money bwana Mac had given her. Despite the anxiety Tururu felt about the part he would inevitably have to play, he liked that his missi usually bested the big bwana. Only thing was, Tururu never knew how she was going to do it, or the toll it would take on him. He took his cues from her.

She headed toward van Zyl and stumbled into a pile of neatly stacked sisal mats, scattering them across the cement floor. Flailing around, she ploughed into a rack of hoes. They rocked back and forth, then fell into place again. She stared at them as if willing them to fall.

"Watch where the hell you are going!" van Zyl yelled.

"Sorree." She motioned to Tururu with a furtive jerk of her head.

He rushed over, shooting an anxious glance at van Zyl.

"Put them back all untidy," she whispered.

She straightened and headed for the display of sweets on the counter, some of them still in the boxes in which they'd been shipped: slabs of Wilson's toffee, Peppermint Crisp, licorice Allsorts, squares of Wicks bubble gum, and puffy bags of coconut-covered marshmallows. A big jar of sherbit sat beside this display, a metal scoop half-buried in the sweet, white powder that prickled when you stuck your tongue in it. Elizabeth's favorite.

Glancing uneasily at her retreating back, Tururu began to stack the mats haphazardly. He didn't like this plan. He was going to get a slap on the head from the bwana for certain. Maybe even something worse.

"The way you found 'em," van Zyl growled, glaring at Tururu.

"Yes, bwana." He continued to stack the mats haphazardly, but a little more slowly this time.

Van Zyl slapped two bars of Sunlight soap on the counter, then lifted out a dripping bottle of milk from an icebox and shoved both items toward Elizabeth. Pinching his cigarette between forefinger and thumb, he took a deep drag, letting the smoke leak from the corners of his mouth. "You want something else, hey?"

Blinking against the smoke, Elizabeth handed him two empty matchboxes. "Um, two matchboxes of sherbit, please, plus an extra shilling's worth. Oh, and a Wilson's toffee . . . and a packet of licorice Allsorts as well."

Tururu grinned to himself. licorice Allsorts were his favorite.

Van Zyl replaced his stub of a cigarette on the counter and took the matchboxes from Elizabeth. He dug each one in turn into the jar of sherbit, leveled them off with a fat, nicotine-stained forefinger, and handed both boxes back to Elizabeth. Peeling a sheet of newspaper off a stack on the counter, he began rolling it into a cone. "Why do you hang around with that *kaffir*, hey?"

Elizabeth didn't answer. Tongue out, she was concentrating on closing the matchboxes without losing any of the sherbit. Or pretending to be.

Van Zyl frowned at her as if trying to decide if she was being rude, then reached into the jar of sherbet and dumped a scoopful into the newspaper cone. He twisted the top, handed it to her, and then plucked a packet of licorice Allsorts from its display box and threw it onto the counter.

Tururu lugged the last mat into place, made a stab at tidying them, then looked over at Elizabeth. What now? She gave him a sidelong glance, meaning that he should join her.

"That'll be three and six," van Zyl said.

Elizabeth slid the money across the counter. "Thank you, Mr. van Zyl."

Tururu sidled up beside Elizabeth. Without warning, she hit his elbow from behind, jamming his hand into the bag of marshmallows on the counter. The bag popped up and fell on the floor.

"What the hell!" Van Zyl lunged at him over the counter.

Tururu jerked back and slammed into the shelves behind him. Tins of corned beef and an assortment of sweets scattered across the floor.

Van Zyl tried to vault over the counter, then faltered halfway and charged toward the opening at the end instead. Tururu spun around and ran toward the door. Missi had really gone and done it this time. The bwana was going to kill him for sure. And if he didn't, there was still the matter of being allowed back into the store in the future. Missi had better get lots of sherbit.

Van Zyl thundered after him. Tururu risked a glance over his shoulder at Elizabeth. She was busy shoveling sherbit into the newspaper cone with great skill and speed. Distracted for a moment by the sight, Tururu stumbled and was almost caught by the bwana, but then he zigzagged and charged out the door. He flew over the steps and ran toward the main road leading toward Gwelo.

Van Zyl lumbered after him, huffing and puffing, for a little ways. Then he bent over, hands on his knees, panting. "I'll get you . . . bloody troublemaker."

———— ⌇⌇ ————

Tururu didn't turn around until he had reached the baobab tree. Darting behind its elephantine trunk, he peered around. No sign of the bwana. He sank down behind one of the giant's massive flared ridges and tried to catch his breath.

"Boo!"

He jumped to his feet and spun around.

She peered at him from behind the ridge, a triumphant grin on her face. Juggling her purchases, she held up the newspaper cone Mr. van Zyl hadn't filled as he should have: it was now filled to the brim. Shaking his head, Tururu fell back against the baobab trunk and slid onto the ground. She plopped down beside him, pulled out the two matchboxes from her pocket, and handed him one.

Now that he was past the danger, the whole thing did seem a little like fun. Tururu grinned and took the box. "Bwana going to kill Tururu."

"He's got to catch you first. Hey, what about your car?"

His car! He'd forgotten. He started to rise.

She grabbed his arm. "We'll get it later. After we've had our sweets and played 'secrets.'"

He settled back against the tree and carefully slid open his matchbox. Sweet white powder puffed out. He stuck his tongue in the confection and waited for the sharp prickle, then smacked his lips. Elizabeth did the same, and they laughed as the sherbit fizzed on their tongues.

They sat in silence until every speck of sherbit had been licked from the corners of their matchboxes. Elizabeth ripped open the packet of Allsorts and gave him half. He popped three of the sweet licorice confections into his mouth and then shoved the rest into his pocket.

Elizabeth rose to her feet. "It's my turn to bury a secret."

In the tradition of the game Elizabeth had learned in her birthplace of Nkana, in Northern Rhodesia, they took turns burying a "treasure" beneath a scrap of glass. This could be anything from a photo fragment or comic strip to a snakeskin fragment or even an animal tooth. The trick was to find the buried "secret" while the other player counted to twenty. Whoever found the most buried "secrets" in five turns got the slab of Wilson's toffee. The best thing about the game was that you could play it anywhere.

Using a stick, she scratched an uneven circle in the dirt in front of the baobab. "Ready?"

Propping his forearm against the trunk, Tururu closed his eyes and counted to ten, like Elizabeth had taught him. "One potato, two potato, three potato . . ."

At ten, he swung around.

"Off you go!" Elizabeth cried. "One potato, two potato . . ."

Head bent, Tururu scoured the ground. At the count of twelve, he noticed a small patch of freshly dug dirt. Dropping to his knees, he began to dig until he reached a curved fragment of green glass.

He grinned with pleasure. "Jez-zuz!"

He'd always envied the small, gold-edged holy cards she'd collected from St. Justin Martyr School in Johannesburg. This was the first time she'd used one in a "secret." He knew of the bwana Jesus from the time a missionary had come to his village. This was the son of their god.

"My best holy card," Elizabeth said.

Tururu retrieved the small picture, brushed off the dirt, and slid it gently into his pocket. Now it was his turn.

He hadn't dug more than a couple of inches into the ground when the ghostly image of his friend Mfuni's ragged corpse appeared in front of him, one half-eaten arm raised in a pleading motion.

"Help me," Mfuni whispered.

"Arrgh!" Tururu jerked upright.

Elizabeth ran over to him. "What is it?"

Dumbstruck, he couldn't answer.

She shook him. "What's wrong?"

Tururu turned and stared blankly at her. Mfuni was dead. Someone had killed him and left his body out on the veld. He had to go to his friend and bury him so he could join the ancestors.

"Turu, please. Tell me."

Tururu jumped to his feet and started toward the road leading to Gwelo.

"Where are you going?"

"Go home, missi. Take milk and soap for medem."

"What about your car?"

He shook his head. He couldn't worry about anything else. He had to go to Mfuni.

Chapter 8

LIZABETH STARED AT TURU'S RETREATING BACK. SHE peered into the hole he'd dug. Nothing there. She glanced up. He was heading toward the beer hall.

Nelson's warning. She couldn't let him go there alone in his strange state.

She ran back to the baobab, grabbed the bottle of milk, stuffed the sherbit-filled newspaper cone down the front of her blouse, and started after Turu. The beer hall lay down a dusty path a little way down the road. She'd have to hurry to catch up to him. With the mood he was in, he'd surely try to lose her if he knew she was following him. She'd have to be very sneaky.

She stared down the narrow dirt road. Its red dirt embankments emptied over the rise. Turu's slight figure was still visible, though he'd started to jog, his head facing resolutely forward. Sticking to the soft, dusty side of the road where there were no punishing rocks, she broke into a run. She had been the fastest in her class back at St. Justin Martyr. He wasn't going to be able to ditch her. She stayed back, ready to drop to the ground if he should turn around.

The air felt heavy. No breeze. All hint of moisture from the earlier rain was gone. The sun baked the top of her head and her breath burned in her throat. Slowing down, she readjusted her grip on the bottle of milk, wiggled the newspaper cone into a more comfortable position, and kept going.

The beer hall appeared a mile or so away across the veld, shimmering in the heat like a vision. Its corrugated iron roof glinted in the sunlight. It looked as if acacia trees were sprouting through the roof. Turu stopped, wiped his forehead, then cut to the left over the embankment and onto a rutted path. She dropped to the ground, panting. Sherbit billowed up. Choking back a sneeze, she reached inside her blouse and crumpled the top more firmly over the cone. She inched up. Turu seemed oblivious to everything but the building ahead.

She glanced at the bottle of milk. She should just abandon it. It was probably about to turn to cream anyway. Her mother's disapproving voice echoed in her head. She'd be in enough trouble coming home late without it, cream or not. Taking a deep breath, she hugged the bottle and rose to her feet.

Turu was way ahead by then. He seemed to be floating above the ground on a cushion of shimmering air. She hurried to catch up. Her feet burned from the hot ground. A breeze rose, carrying with it the familiar, pungent odor of rotted sorghum: *kaffir* beer. Her stomach growled and she felt light-headed. She should've listened to her mother and eaten a proper lunch.

She glanced up in time to see Turu disappear behind the beer hall, a plain brick building not much bigger than their house. She slowed to a crouching walk and scanned the area. The place seemed deserted. The BSAP—British South African Police— opened the beer hall only on Friday and Saturday nights so the locals wouldn't get drunk every night.

Overgrown hibiscus bushes to the left of the building hugged a low mud wall. In front, a burlap bag filled with sorghum dangled from the branch of an acacia tree. She glanced at the beer hall's heavy, wooden front door. No big padlock on it like the beer halls up in Northern Rhodesia. What was to stop the troublemakers from going in there any old time they wanted to? What if they were in there right now, drinking like fishes and getting more and more riled up over Federation?

She dropped to one knee. She was all alone in the middle of nowhere. What had possessed her to follow Turu? She gripped the milk bottle tighter, ready to use it as a club. Taking a deep breath, she hunched over, charged to the back corner of the building, and pressed herself against the wall. It felt hot against her cheek. She inched her nose around the corner.

The large dirt courtyard around the back was deserted save for a number of upturned buckets that served as seats for the drinkers. A lopsided kitchen chair lolled beside a fire pit, along with a lumpy mattress spread out behind it. Beyond that, another acacia tree.

A hand gripped her shoulder.

She shrieked and spun around, dropping the bottle of milk. It bounced, sending a stream of milk in the air.

"Turu!"

"Sshht!" He pulled her down and glanced around.

"You made me drop the milk," she whispered. "My mom's going to kill me . . . us."

He looked uncertain for a moment, then glared at her.

"What's going on?" she said.

"Why missi follow Tururu?"

"I—I was afraid you'd get into trouble." She felt a little silly saying the words, but it was true.

He glanced around, his eyes bright with fear. "Stupid missi."

"Don't you call me stupid," she said, even though she half thought he was right. She wished she were home.

"Tururu go now. Stay here."

"Where are you going?"

"Tururu come back now-now, take missi home."

"But—"

"No, missi!" He gave her a fierce glare and charged around the wall.

Elizabeth sank to the ground and hugged herself. Maybe she should just run home. But what if she encountered someone coming this way? Plus, she wasn't even sure which way home was, or even how to get back to Mr. van Zyl's shop. Tears pricked her eyes. Turu was right. This was a stupid thing to do.

With shaking hands, she picked up the bottle of milk, threw back the last of it, and rose to her feet. She couldn't just sit there. She had to do something.

Strains of a strange chant filled the air. She peered around the wall. Turu, partially shielded by the acacia's trunk, kneeled in the dirt, arms outstretched to the sky. Praying the way *muntus* did. She'd seen him do it before. Glancing around, she ran to the tree and risked a peek.

A dead body lay sprawled halfway out of a shallow grave, one of its arms all chewed up. Through a film of buzzing flies, she could tell that the figure was that of a slight young man wearing shorts and a filthy, bloodstained shirt. His face was bloated and caked with dirt.

She gagged and turned away. When she looked back, Turu was ripping a stick holding a small, crude bag with feathers sticking out of it from the ground near the foot of the grave. Some African hocus-pocus thing. Shouting something she couldn't understand, he lobbed the contraption angrily across the veld. It looped in the air, then fell some distance away. He watched it fall, then turned back toward the body and stood staring down at it, making soft tch-tch sounds. He was crying.

She whispered his name.

Wiping his eyes, Turu dragged the body behind a bush a couple of yards away, where he covered it with branches. He reached into the pouch around his neck, removed a handful of dark powder, and scattered it over the body, all the while muttering a stream of words. The only word Elizabeth could make out was the name: Mfuni.

Mfuni! Her dad's missing boss boy. Glancing around, Turu caught sight of her. He frowned.

"Tururu tell missi to wait there." He jabbed his finger toward the other end of the beer hall.

"What happened to him?"

"We go home now." He turned and headed toward the veld.

She ran to catch up and fell in step beside him. It was easier without worrying about the milk. "That's the worker my dad's been looking for, isn't it?"

He stopped, alarm on his face. "No tell bwana."

"Why not?"

"Big *indaba* for all *muntu*."

"Come on. Why would *all* of you get into big trouble?"

"Please, missi, do not tell bwana."

"Maybe my dad can find out who did it. Wouldn't you like that?"

"Tururu . . . Tururu make magic for missi if you don't tell bwana."

"Uh, that's all right." She glanced down at the grubby pouch hanging around his neck. She'd probably have to swallow some disgusting potion made out of ground-up eland dung and snake teeth, or something. She looked up at his familiar face. He seemed so scared. "I won't tell."

Flashing her a look of gratitude, he started walking again.

"Do you have any money? We'd better go buy more milk and get the soap I forgot. We can get your car at the same time." She pulled out her change. "I just need a tickey."

Turu dug into his pocket and removed chunks of glass and several crumpled images cut from newspapers, along with five pennies. She took three of them.

"We've got to hurry," she said. "Madam give missi big *indaba*."

Turu nodded anxiously and started to jog toward the path and van Zyl's shop. She trotted beside him.

"By the way, what's that circle around Mfuni and that stuff you sprinkled on him supposed to do?"

"Make Mfuni invisible."

"Honestly?" She gave him a fond grin.

He nodded. Once they were clear of the building, she couldn't resist glancing over her shoulder.

She blinked. There was no sign of the body.

Chapter 9

THAT NIGHT TURURU RETURNED TO THE BEER HALL, carrying bwana Mac's spade. He headed toward the island of light behind the beer hall and the shouts of drunken men. He'd been so anxious about the task ahead he hadn't timed it quite right. He'd have to wait until the beer hall closed. He glanced up at the sky. At least there was no moon tonight.

Crouching over, he ran to the hibiscus bush farthest into the shadows and eased down between the bush and the low mud wall. Shivering in the cool night air, he peered around the wall toward the back of the beer hall. Karari was coming down the back steps, headed toward the fire pit, followed by Tutenda, a sisal worker, Chipo, and Nelson. They all carried emptied baked bean tins filled with beer. Tururu fought the impulse to bolt. He couldn't put off burying his friend. The man's spirit would drive him mad.

Angling ahead of the others, Tutenda plunked one of the overturned buckets in front of Karari, spilling half his beer in the process.

Karari was about to sit. Then he froze and turned toward the acacia tree. "Where's Mfuni?"

The three men stared blankly at one another.

Karari glared at Nelson. "Anesu!"

Shrinking back, Nelson shook his head rapidly.

Karari considered him for a moment, took a sip of beer, then sank down onto the overturned bucket Tutenda had placed for him. Elbows on his knees, he gazed into the fire. A whisper rose from the coals. He smiled and crooked his finger in a beckoning motion. The embers came to life, began to curl into a blue wave, and rose toward him. But then, as if changing his mind, he lifted his hand in a stopping motion and the wave sank back down.

Tururu gasped. Karari's powers were growing.

The men glanced furtively at one another.

"I will destroy you if you cross me." Karari gave each man a meaningful stare. "You understand?"

Three heads bobbed in agreement.

Karari held out his hand to Tutenda. "*Ubuthi.*"

Tutenda fumbled in his shorts pocket, withdrew a worn brown packet, and handed it to Karari. Tururu gasped. Bwana Mac's poison.

"You trained your bird well," Karari said. "Our people will remember this."

Tutenda clapped his hands softly and bowed his head. "It is my honor."

Karari handed his beer to Chipo and removed a dented snuff tin from his pocket. He filled it with the powder from the brown packet and then held it out to Nelson. "Do not fail this time."

Head bowed, Nelson took the snuff tin with both hands. Tururu could feel his father's fear. "But the bwana, he lock—"

Karari walloped Nelson on the side of his head, sending him sprawling. The tin flew from his hand and landed near Karari's foot. A few heads turned, some laughter with no humor in it.

Karari scooped up the tin, grabbed Nelson by the front of his shirt, and shoved it against Nelson's chest. "No excuses. They *will* all die."

Nelson slipped the tin into his shirt pocket. "Yes, *n'anga*."

"*Godobori!*"

"*Godobori.*"

Karari punched both fists in the air. "Death to our enemies!"

"Death to our enemies!" the group repeated in croaking voices.

Joseph Kachambwa, a burly Bantu auxiliary policeman, appeared in the back doorway of the beer hall, clanging a huge, spit-polished brass bell. "Time!" He stared pointedly in their direction and then turned and strode back into the beer hall, still ringing the bell. Everyone had five minutes to clear out. And clear out they always did. No one ever ignored Joseph Kachambwa's call. To do so would mean a bloody nose, or worse.

Karari stared at the policeman's back with a look on his face that suggested he might risk it. But then he turned back to his companions—all stood as if at attention.

Karari turned to Nelson. "Come to my hut when you have done the job. And know this: they die, or you will." He turned back to the fire and, without looking at the three men, flapped a dismissive hand in their direction. The men scattered.

Tururu remained still as a rock as his father passed less than five feet away from his hiding place before melting into the night. Despite himself, he felt sorry for his father. He was also very afraid for Elizabeth.

Karari stood staring down at the fire, a satisfied smirk on his face. But then, as if remembering the missing body, his head snapped back toward where Mfuni lay, safe beneath Tururu's spell. His smile faded. Then, like a lion catching the scent of buck, he lifted his chin and cast a puzzled glance about him. His gaze came to rest on Tururu's hiding place.

Amai Vedu! Karari could see him. Tururu recited every protective sacred word he knew.

Karari stopped and shook his head, and then, with a last glance toward where Mfuni's body had lain, headed toward the *kraal*.

Tururu waited until everybody cleared out and Joseph Kachambwa had locked up. He waited another half an hour, in case Karari returned. Then he buried Mfuni beneath a wattle tree a short distance from the beer hall and disguised the grave as best he could with what magic he knew. His friend was now safe with the ancestors.

Hefting the spade over his shoulder, he started back toward home. He couldn't wait to crawl into bed. His father had had enough to drink; he wouldn't have noticed his absence.

Grandmother's image popped into his mind, and he stopped. She was calling to him.

He turned and hurried across the veld, toward the black monkey thorn tree where he usually called forth Grandmother's hut. It was so dark he could barely see where he was going, but his feet knew the way. Panting, he arrived at the tree. Without catching his breath, he called forth an image of her hut as he usually did.

It appeared in moments, as if it had been there all along, the blue flames of the *ngozi* visible in front. He hurried inside, dropped the spade, and fell to his knees beside Grandmother's pallet.

"You came," she whispered.

In the glow from the fire outside, Tururu could see that her bandage had been changed. His mother's work. She must've slipped from their *kiya* after he left for the beer hall.

"What does Grandmother need?" he asked.

"Your mother meant well, but I need more of the *muti* you made before. The wound is not healing as I expected. We must stop the *ngozi* poison."

He jumped to his feet, lit a candle, and quickly went about mixing the ingredients, double-checking with Grandmother as he did. A short while later, he'd made a fresh batch of the mixture and replaced her bandage. She gave a sigh and the pain in her face eased. He sank back down beside her pallet.

She looked up at him. "What is it, Tur—Sabata? Tell me, what has happened?"

He told her everything.

"Mfuni," she whispered. "I couldn't tell it was him. But I knew in my heart Karari was the killer."

"Mfuni is with the ancestors now."

"You were very brave."

"Grandmother must stop my father."

"I must rise from my bed to save the whites?"

"But the *picannin dona* . . . I will help you mix—"

"No. And you, Sabata, you must not interfere. This is not our fight."

Tururu bit his lip. His face settled into a stubborn frown. He would have to save the *picannin* missi himself.

"No, I tell you, Sabata! Let the *picannin dona* turn to her white god for help. You cannot go against Karari. You are not ready."

He sagged.

She patted his cheek. "Go now. Grandmother must rest. We will do what Amai Vedu tells us."

"Yes, Grandmother." He kissed her damp forehead and rose to his feet.

She clasped his hand and held his gaze. "Stay out of it."

He nodded and left with a heavy heart. What was he to do?

Chapter 10

ELIZABETH DRAGGED HERSELF OUT OF BED AN HOUR LATER than usual. She'd hardly slept. Every time she dozed off, she found herself back at the beer hall in the pitch of night, petrified, unable to tell which way was home. Small black creatures kept popping up out of the ground, trying to grab her. At one point, Mfuni burst out of nowhere as she was running from the creatures and seized her by the foot. Another time he was sitting in a grave, staring at her, half his face missing.

She'd considered crawling into bed with her parents, but was afraid the nightmare would start all over again—and then what if she accidentally said something? There would be questions. At first light, she rose and stumbled down the hallway, past her parents' darkened bedroom. She had to find Turu.

Nelson's raspy voice came from the kitchen. "Everywhere I turn, you are there. What is the matter with you?"

"Nothing, father," Turu whispered back.

She entered the kitchen. Nelson stood at the stove, smacking a wooden spoon against the side of a pot of simmering porridge. Turu hovered barely a foot away, watching him.

"Turu," Elizabeth said, "I-I need you to help me with something." Before Nelson could protest, she grabbed Turu's arm and tugged him toward the door. A glance over her shoulder revealed that for once Nelson seemed only too pleased to be rid of his son.

"Not now, missi. I must stay with father."

"Why?"

He shook his head and glanced back over his shoulder at his father like he was trying to catch him at something.

"Come on. I need to talk to you." Trusting him to follow, she headed for the wheelbarrow and dropped down behind it. With one last glance in his father's direction, he sank down beside her.

"What, missi?"

"We've got to tell somebody about Mfuni's—"

"No, missi!"

"Listen, somebody killed him. It's just too awful. My dad said he was a good boy."

"I tell you, missi—"

"Okay, here's what I'll do. I'll just tell my dad. No one else. I-I'll tell him I was out for a walk, and . . . I came across the body, or something. I'll leave you out of it—"

"Missi promised!"

"But what about the people who killed him? Don't you want them caught and punished?"

"Mfuni with ancestors. Bwana cannot change anything. Missi promised."

She considered him for a long moment. Something more was going on than just being afraid he'd get into trouble with the bwanas. Turu never asked anything of her. Maybe she should just stay out of it.

"Oh, all right. I won't tell, then."

His shoulders sagged in relief.

"By the way, did you tell your grand—" She broke off at the sound of a car approaching and peered over the edge of the wheelbarrow.

In a whirling cloud of dust, Mr. Bradley's truck was headed their way. Turu jumped up and, in a crouch, took off for the bottom of the yard like a spooked duiker buck. The truck swerved into the driveway and stopped inches from the back of the Ford. That was just how Mr. Bradley did things. In the bed of the truck—with the three Bradley boys—were toddler-size sacks of flour and sugar, bottles of beer, gin, brandy, and other provisions packed in big wooden boxes. The door swung open and Mr. Bradley stepped out, a cigarette dangling from the corner of his mouth. He stretched, revealing a roll of hairy belly between his khaki shirt and shorts.

Elizabeth dropped back down behind the wheelbarrow. Her face blazed at the thought of the boys seeing her in her pajamas. But she couldn't stay where she was. Any minute now they would spread out looking for something to break or torture and see her huddled behind the wheelbarrow. Taking a deep breath, she rose to her feet, clutched her arms around her waist, and, focusing on the kitchen door, walked as fast as she could toward the house.

"Elizabeth!" Mr. Bradley called. "How's my girl?"

"Uh, hello, Mr. Bradley," Elizabeth said, without stopping. "I'm very well, thank you."

From the corner of her eye, she could see three heads swivel her way. Miraculously, the boys were still in the truck, their backs to the cab. Andre and Clive wore smirks. Ian drew back his pretend slingshot and eyed her along its length. Elizabeth put her head down and quickened her pace.

"Hey, Lloyd. What are you doing here so early?"

Elizabeth glanced up. Her father, barefoot and clad in an old pair of shorts and his pajama top, squinted groggily at Mr. Bradley from the doorway. He held a cup of tea in his hand. He threw Elizabeth a puzzled glance.

"I thought I'd drop everything off on my way to pick up that lamb I had slaughtered," Mr. Bradley said. "This way we can get everything in the bins before everybody gets here."

"Good idea."

"I brought the boys to help."

Elizabeth started up the back steps and slipped past her father, into the house. Nelson stood at the sink. Reaching into the sideboard, she retrieved a bowl, helped herself to porridge, dumped in butter and sugar, then stood by the window eating and watching the boys. They hardly ever came inside the house, but you just never knew with them. Mr. Bradley and her father chatted about all the stuff Mr. Bradley had bought in Gwelo the day before, how bad the roads were, and the sisal-processing machine her dad had fixed.

"Come on, boys," Mr. Bradley called. They straggled to their feet, stretching and yawning.

"Elizabeth!"

She swung around. Her mother, clad in her dressing gown, stood at the kitchen table frowning at her. "What've I told you about bolting down your food? Now sit down at the table and eat properly."

Elizabeth took a last bite and set the bowl in the sink. "Finished."

Her mother shook her head. "Cup of tea please, Nelson."

"Yes, medem."

"Be out in a moment, as soon as I put my shoes on." Her father turned back into the house.

"By the way," Mr. Bradley called. "Thanks for volunteering to drive Emily to the station."

Her mother did a slow turn toward her father.

He didn't meet her eyes. Instead he turned on his heel and headed for their bedroom. "Um, glad to help out."

Her mother watched him go, her eyes smoldering. What now?

Her father must have lied about Mr. Bradley asking him to drive Mrs. Bradley to the station. She blushed inside for him. There would be another argument. She hurried to her bedroom to change.

Minutes later, dressed in shorts and an old blouse, Elizabeth peeked through the kitchen curtains for any sign of the Bradley boys. They were helping her father and Mr. Bradley haul provisions from the truck to the storeroom. She hurried to the front of the house and slipped out the front door. She shivered.

She should've brought a jersey, but she wasn't going back into the house—not with the mood her mother was in. Besides, she didn't want to be trapped into taking tea with the Bradleys. She never knew what those dreadful boys were going to do under the table.

She searched for Turu in a couple of his old hiding places: behind the blue gum trees, where he took naps on a cushion from the Bradleys' old couch, and the drainage ditch in front of the house, where he sometimes smoked his dad's awful *stompies*. But he was nowhere to be found.

By then it was around ten o'clock. She could hear her father and the Bradleys moving things around in the storeroom. She waited behind the garage until they had locked the storeroom and were all safely in the house for tea, including the Bradley boys. She hurried over to the avocado tree and climbed up to the half-built tree house she and Turu had started a couple of months earlier. It consisted of three different lengths of plank nailed above a fork halfway up the tree, creating a floor of sorts. The thick foliage made it all but invisible from the ground.

Reaching the tree house, she crawled across the plank and leaned back against the tree fork. As soon as the Bradleys cleared out, Turu would show up. Although . . . now that she had seen what he could do with his magic, she suspected he might be hiding just a few feet away, watching her.

A flicker of movement near the morning glory–strangled fence caught her eye, and she sat up. A gangly native was crouching in front of the fence, gazing at the storeroom. Elizabeth flattened herself against the tree house floor and peered through a gap in the planks. Glancing around, the man drew himself up, closed his eyes, and muttered something. In moments his entire body began to waver like a mirage on the veld. He started to drift, up, up into the air, becoming more and more ghostlike as he rose.

The thing hung there for a moment, vibrating. But then, with a pop and a shimmer, the ghostly figure turned back into a man and dropped to earth. Elizabeth rubbed her eyes. When she opened them again, the man was on his feet, desperately twirling his arms in the air. Moments later, he turned back into the same apparition as before and veered into the air. The thing dived and soared and wheeled around in the air for a few moments, and then—like that hawk eagle from a couple of days before—plunged back to earth, this time with a purpose. It headed straight for the storeroom wall.

Like a wisp of smoke through a sheet, it disappeared into the building.

Stunned, Elizabeth lay there, her heart doing flip-flops.

What just happened? Had she imagined the whole thing?

She scrambled down the tree and headed toward the house for the storeroom key. A faint hissing sound coming from the storeroom stopped her. Dropping to the ground in a crouch, she turned to see that same ghostly figure filter out through the middle of the door. And then, as if sensing her presence, the figure hung in the air and turned a pair of piercing, disembodied eyes toward her. She couldn't tear her gaze away.

Time froze.

And then the thing was gone.

Shaking uncontrollably, she tried to gather her wits.

"What on earth are you doing?" her father called.

She swung around. Her father, Mr. Bradley, and the three boys stood near the back step staring at her. Forcing herself to be calm, she pretended to scratch at something in the ground. Her hands shook. "Um, I uh . . . think there's a shilling half-buried in the ground here."

"Mine!" Andre called.

"Oh, shut up, you scamming little bugger," Mr. Bradley said with a grin. He clipped his son lightly across the back of the head and turned to her father. "Well, I'd better be off, then."

"Hurry back. We've got some beer to drink."

Mr. Bradley headed for the truck followed by the boys, who scrapped all the way there and then tried to stop one another from climbing in. With Clive running next to the truck, trying to hoist himself in, and the other two slapping at his hands and head, Mr. Bradley backed down the driveway. Clive finally managed to get one leg in by the time Mr. Bradley turned onto the road. He hung onto the side as the truck sped toward the Bradley house.

Elizabeth couldn't help a shaky grin.

"Psst!"

Elizabeth swung around. Turu emerged from behind the back of the storeroom wall.

"Oh, Turu!" She hurried toward him. "I'm so glad to see you. You won't believe what I just—"

"Hey, Tururu!" her father called. "Come help Nelson carry in supplies."

He and Nelson were headed toward the storeroom carrying the "house" storage jars, which would be filled from the main supply. Neither Nelson nor Turu was allowed in the storeroom without her father.

"Yes, bwana." Turu hurried toward the two men. He glanced back at Elizabeth with a puzzled look.

Elizabeth followed. She'd have to tell him later what she'd seen, but now she was going to check inside the storeroom for signs of the . . . thing. What could it possibly have been doing in there?

"You missed tea with the Bradleys," her father said with a sly smile as he handed Turu the jar he'd been carrying.

Forcing herself to be normal, Elizabeth cleared her throat and said in her best cheeky voice, "I hope they didn't get any ladyfingers."

Grinning at her, he unlocked the door and stepped inside. "That would be like giving ice cream to pigs, don't you think?"

She laughed and followed him inside while he took back the jars and set them on the floor. Turu and Nelson waited outside. Elizabeth glanced around, hoping there were no dead rats. She couldn't take anything more just then.

"Did you manage to get your shilling?" Holding the house flour jar, her father lifted the flour-bin lid and reached in for the scoop.

"Shilling?"

"The one you were scratching for earlier."

"Um . . ." She peered in the sugar and cornmeal bins.

"What are you looking for?"

"Uh, nothing. Just looking."

He scooped flour into the jar. "What schemes have you got going this time?"

"Just the tree house, the sweet peas—oh, and the swimming pool."

"I wish you'd put things away when you start something." He handed her the filled flour jar. "Give that to Nelson, would you please?"

"Elizabeth!" her mother called.

"Coming!" She kissed her father on the cheek, hurried out, and handed the container to Nelson. She tried to catch Turu's eye, but he seemed preoccupied.

"So that's where you were." Her mother stood in the kitchen doorway shading her eyes. Her hair was pulled back into a loose knot at the nape of her neck, making her face look even more drawn. "I want you to tidy your bedroom and then help me with the flowers. There's a good girl. Nelson is going to be too busy baking bread to help."

Elizabeth trudged to the back door and was about to follow her mother into the house when she heard Nelson give a shrill, panicked cry.

She swung around to see Turu sprinting away with what appeared to be a snuff tin in his hand. Nelson stared after him with a stunned expression. Puzzled by such blatant disobedience, she watched Turu disappear through the opening between the blue gum trees and the fence.

He was going to catch hell later. What did he think was so important that it was worth it?

A couple of hours later, after finishing her chores, Elizabeth headed for the kitchen. Her father was in the front yard tidying the area around Elizabeth's "swimming pool," a half-dug hole, so far. The house was filled with the mouthwatering odor of baking bread. Her stomach growled. They were supposed to be having leftover macaroni and cheese for lunch, but she wanted fresh, hot bread, right out of the oven. She didn't want to have to wait until the evening's *braai*. Besides, stolen bread always tasted better.

She didn't care what her mother said or did; she was going to swipe some of that crispy bread immediately. She would pinch enough for Turu, who was hiding from Nelson in the tree house. She would probably be sneaking food to him until Nelson calmed down, which might take a long time. He'd been acting jumpy and nervous all morning. After what she'd seen, so had she.

She headed down the hallway toward the kitchen. Her mother stood at the cabinet with her back to Elizabeth. Nelson hunched over the sink, scrubbing a pot like a madman. The way he was carrying on, you'd swear Turu had stolen more than just a stupid tin of snuff. Three loaves of crusty bread lay on a flour sack on the counter. She tiptoed over and tore off two chunks of the loaf closest to her. Juggling the hot bread in her hands, she turned and started to tiptoe outside.

"Elizabeth!" her mother cried from the hallway.

Elizabeth charged through the back door and flew down the steps toward the blue gum trees, stuffing a piece of bread into her mouth as she ran. Chewing, she glanced over her shoulder, swallowed, and tripped over the rooster. She sprawled on the ground in front of the coop and Turu's chunk of bread flew from her hand. With a loud squawk, the rooster slashed at her leg with its beak and charged away. Pookie darted from the coop and pecked furiously at the bread.

"Ow!" She sat up to check her leg. There was an angry red welt just above her ankle.

"Serves you right," her mother called from the back steps. "Now get back in here and clean yourself up."

She turned on her heel and stalked back into the kitchen.

Elizabeth spat on her fingers and dabbed at the wound. From the corner of her eye, she could see Turu grinning at her from one of the lower branches of the tree. She turned and made a face at him, then pointed toward Pookie, who was still pecking away at the piece of bread she'd dropped.

That was your piece, she mouthed. *How funny is that, smarty-pants?*

Pookie squawked, a funny, strangled sound. She swung around in time to see him keel over and lie there without moving.

"Pookie!" She scrambled to her feet.

A spasm of searing pain tore through her own stomach. She gasped and doubled over, trying to suck air into her lungs. It felt like a giant hand was squeezing her stomach into a tiny ball.

"Missi!" Turu dropped from the tree and ran toward her. He gripped her elbow and tried to pull her to her feet. She fell, and he yanked her back on her feet. "Come quickly."

She tried to wrench her arm away. "What're you doing?"

"Missi will die." He slipped his shoulder under hers and half dragged her along. "Must hurry."

"Where are you taking—" But she couldn't concentrate. It felt like someone was cutting her stomach into shreds.

"Tururu!" a voice cried from a far off distance.

Mom?

"What the hell are you doing?"

Elizabeth tried to find her feet, tried to focus. Her neck felt stiff and she couldn't stop twitching. As if in a dream, she became dimly aware of being on the ground by the tap with Turu tearing at the pouch around his neck and her mother screaming her name. And then she was being carried. She passed out.

Chapter 11

TURURU SAT ON THE OLD COUCH CUSHION BEHIND THE blue gum trees, his head in his hands. How had his father managed to poison the flour even *after* he stole the snuff tin? Maybe he'd hidden a portion of it somewhere in the kitchen. He shook his head. That didn't seem likely.

He bolted upright.

Karari! It would be just like him to make sure. Karari didn't trust anyone. But how and when? In Gwelo? Impossible. On bwana Bradley's truck? Never, not with those picannin bwanas around. Somehow, he must've sneaked into the storeroom.

Tururu's only hope now was the white doctor. Any minute now, bwana Mac would return with bwana Goodwin. He glanced up at the sun. But where were they? He rose to his feet and started pacing.

What if missi was already dead? He had to see for himself.

With his heart threatening to burst from his chest, he glanced around and headed toward the front of the house. Gripping the window ledge outside Elizabeth's bedroom window, he inched up to peek through.

She lay sprawled across the bed, strands of hair plastered around her face. The mosquito net, attached to the ceiling by a hook, dangled above her in a big knot. Medem sat beside the bed wiping missi's face. A half-filled bowl of water sat on the nightstand next to her.

Missi's eyes flew open and her body arched. She was the same color as the white sheets.

Tururu ducked down. At least she was still alive, but it wouldn't be long now. Tururu knew he would have to save her.

He sneaked back around the house. His father was in the kitchen, working at the sink by the window. Keeping low, he charged into their *kiya* and grabbed a cup, an enamel bowl, and his mother's pestle from the table, then ran toward the tap on the other side of the house where he couldn't be seen. He dropped beside the tap, set out his utensils, and removed the pouch from around his neck.

Now to remember what ingredients he'd need for missi's kind of poisoning. And how much of each ingredient? Grandmother always made it look so easy—a little of this, a little of that, almost without thought. Why hadn't he paid more attention? Too little of this or too much of that would be no good at all, maybe even make missi worse.

His mind was all jumbled up. He couldn't do this alone. He reached for his amulet and closed his eyes.

Please, Amai Vedu, help this worthless apprentice save missi.

He waited for inspiration, a voice in his ear, some kind of sign from above.

Nothing.

He opened his eyes and sat staring at the ground. The only thing he could do was to make a potion by listening to the voice in his heart. Missi's life depended on it.

Taking a deep breath, he broke off a thumbnail-size piece of the herb used to cure poisoning in cattle and threw it into the bowl. That felt right. A pinch of bee pollen—to repair her stomach—felt right too. He threw in another pinch. Missi ate a lot, she had a big stomach. He added charcoal to absorb the poison. He couldn't go wrong there. A sprig of the roselle plant to help missi's blood pump out the poison. And then he was done.

Or was he?

He stared down at the vile-looking mixture. He said another prayer and waited. Nothing. No voice telling him what to do, like it did for Grandmother. Maybe it was because he was finished. Using his mother's pestle, he ground the concoction as fine as he could, then added just enough water so missi could drink the *muti*. He stirred the murky contents with his finger until everything was blended, then poured it all into the cup. He licked his finger and gagged.

Giving a shudder, he rose to his feet and headed for Elizabeth's bedroom window, cup in hand. He would retrieve his mother's utensils later, after he had cured missi.

He glanced uneasily toward his grandmother's hut. She'd told him this was not his fight, to let missi trust to the white doctor and the white god. But the white doctor wasn't here, and as for the white god, who knew?

Surely Grandmother wouldn't be too mad at him for trying to save his friend. He would make her understand later.

When he peeked back into missi's bedroom, she was lying on her back, a folded white cloth over her forehead. Her breath came in quick, shallow gasps. Medem sat by her side, rocking back and forth, a handkerchief pressed to her lips. Tururu watched in dismay. How was he going to get medem out of the room? He considered banging on the back door, and then when medem went to answer it, he could run back. But then what about his father?

Wait. Medem was rising to her feet. With an anxious glance at Elizabeth, she slipped from the room.

Thank you, Amai Vedu. Tururu climbed through the window. Cup in hand, he headed for the bed.

"Missi," he whispered, one eye on the door.

Her eyelids were purple. They stayed shut. How was he going to do this?

He leaned over her. "Wake up. Drink *muti*."

She didn't move.

Angling his body sideways, Tururu tugged her jaw down with one hand, tilted the cup in his other hand, and slowly poured a quarter of the contents into her mouth.

She jerked up in some kind of spasm, spluttered, swallowed, and then sank back down again, her mouth and neck streaked with dark stains.

Glancing at the door, Tururu made a feeble attempt to wipe her chin with the bottom of his shirt. He continued to pour the remaining *muti* into her mouth. He paused. She just laid there, the pool of liquid rising and falling with each breath she took.

"Please, missi. Please drink."

"Tururu!" Medem stood in the doorway. "What the hell—"

Tururu stared at her in frozen horror.

She charged toward him. "What did you just give her?"

"*Muti*," Tururu cried. "Tururu fix *picannin* missi—"

"If she dies, I swear—"

Dropping the cup, Tururu turned and dove through the window. He hit the ground and didn't stop running until he was halfway across the veld.

What if he'd killed his friend with his so-called remedy? His father was right. He was a worthless *n'anga*. He couldn't even mix a simple remedy for poisoning. He could never be *godobori*. He prayed Grandmother would help him save missi. It was up to Amai Vedu now. And perhaps the white god.

Exhausted, Tururu finally reached the black monkey thorn tree. All around him, the lowering darkness had turned the veld into shadows and shifting shapes. The acrid smell of evening fires hung in the air. Catching his breath, he closed his eyes and called out to his grandmother with his heart and mind.

But when he opened his eyes, the hut hadn't appeared like it usually did.

Heart pounding, he dropped to the ground and glanced around. Did Karari have something to do with this? He rose into a crouch. Or was Grandmother teaching him a lesson for trying to save his friend?

Drawing himself up, he quieted his heart and closed his eyes again. Focusing, he called out to her again, took a deep breath, and opened his eyes.

The hut was there, in its usual spot. And there was Grandmother on her three-legged stool, staring down at the ground in front of her. But instead of sitting in her usual spot beside the fire, she now squatted near the doorway. She was keeping her distance from the *ngozi* until she healed, at which time she would take full command of them, as before. Tururu started down the incline. Grandmother's *douk* was on her head again. A good sign. She had to be feeling better. But why wasn't she looking in his direction like she usually did, always aware of his arrival?

He stopped a short distance in front of her. She hadn't even sensed his approach. Her focus was on her scattered magic bones: yellowed pieces from a lion's paw, antelope tail, and the jawbone of a hyena. They told her of places and events she couldn't always see with her spirit eye. He noticed with alarm how drawn her face looked—even worse than before.

"Grandmother?"

Her head snapped up. "Tururu! I did not hear you. Come, come." She motioned for him to join her, then gazed back down at the bones.

She'd called him Tururu. Something *was* wrong. He dropped to his knees in the dirt beside her.

She swung around and stared at him, her gaze sharp with concern. "What is it?"

This was his usual grandmother. Without looking at her, he quickly explained what had happened, ending with, "You must help save my—"

Before he could get the last word out, she whacked him across the side of his head.

"What did Anesu tell Sabata about interfering, eh?

He rubbed his head, aware he was at least Sabata again. "But you will help missi?"

"No."

"But missi will die!"

She shrugged and turned from him. "Let this be a lesson to you. Now perhaps you will pay closer attention to your lessons, eh? And to what Grandmother says."

"But Grandmother promised me that missi would not die."

"This was not my doing."

Tururu's shoulders slumped.

She considered him for a moment, and her face softened. "Very well, I will make *muti*. I will try to save your Missi. But I cannot promise anything."

He stared at her in alarm. "But Grandmother, your *muti* always works."

She held up her bandaged hand. "Everything has changed. Anesu can no longer see anything in the bones. I don't know what will happen with my other powers. I am weak."

"What will you do?"

Drawing in a deep breath, she set her jaw. "Right now, I will try to save your Missi. We will then see how my magic is working. But you must help." She lumbered to her feet and hobbled into the hut.

Tururu hurried after her and took her arm. They headed for the table where she usually mixed her potions. Lined up at the back of it was a haphazard assortment of used gherkin, mayonnaise, and jam jars filled with various powders, liquids, and parts of various things. A curtain of dried herbs hung from the ceiling. With a grunt, Grandmother hefted herself onto her stool and then reached for an old stone bowl stained with chicken blood. She placed it in front of her. Tururu lit the paraffin lamp and stood beside her.

She gave him a pointed look. "Pay attention, this time."

"Yes, Grandmother." He edged closer and watched while she reached for one jar after another, eyeballing amounts of powders, bits of insects, and snippets from the herbs hanging above. With each addition she tossed in the bowl, she explained how much and why, then made him repeat everything after her. Tururu's mind went fuzzy like it usually did at moments like these, more so now because he was anxious.

"Now I need something that belongs to the little Missi," Grandmother said. "Anything will do."

His heart sank. He didn't have anything of hers. Did this mean he would have to run back to the bwanas' house and risk—? Then he remembered missi's picture of their god, Jesus, the one he'd uncovered when they played "secrets." He reached into his pocket. It was still there!

He held it out to Grandmother. "It's a picture of their god."

Grandmother's eyebrows went up. "Very good. Burn it. The ashes go into the bowl." She shambled outside, carrying a small gourd.

Tururu gave the card one last, regretful look, then set it on fire over the bowl. He watched it curl and dance into a whisper of gray ash that drifted over the rest of the mixture.

Grandmother returned and added a pinch of dried lumanda and then a generous portion of ground charcoal.

"I used that one in missi's mixture," he said.

She tilted the bowl toward him. "This much?"

His face fell. "Less."

Clucking her tongue, she reached for her knife. "Sabata knows what Anesu needs now."

Tururu held out his finger.

With a practiced flick of the knife, she pierced his fingertip. He held his finger over the bowl and watched his blood drip into it.

"That is enough." She began to grind the mixture into a lumpy consistency with her pestle before dumping the contents onto a square of faded cloth.

She motioned for him to tie the ends together. When he was done, she drew herself up and closed her eyes. Extending both hands over the bundle, she began to chant—but then broke off with a cry of pain and clutched her bad arm above the bandage.

"What is it?"

"Burning. Hot. So hot." Grandmother threw back her head. "Fire in my bones."

"Tururu make more *muti*?"

"No time. You must help me. Give me your strength."

Hugging her bad hand to her chest, she took his hand with her good one, closed her eyes, and held it over the bundle.

Tururu felt a rush of energy pass through her hand, but the force of it was not as strong as it had been in the past. And there was something about it that made him uneasy. He glanced at her closed eyes and felt her struggling. With the *ngozi*? Or with something else? He shivered. But he trusted his grandmother. She was strong. She would make it right.

He closed his eyes and forced himself to become still. Grandmother began the incantation once again. When her voice faltered, Tururu took up the chant, using words he didn't even know he knew.

Their voices rose and blended. The air crackled.

"It is done," Grandmother said. Tururu opened his eyes. She was staring at him with an expression of approval. "Well done, Sabata."

Tururu gave a shy grin. "I-I didn't even know—

"I needed you." She held out her good arm. "Help me to my bed. I must lie down."

He helped her across the room. "I will make more *muti*."

She nodded, eased down onto her mattress, and fell back. Tururu hurried over to the table, mixed the poultice with practiced ease, and returned.

"You must hurry," Grandmother said as he applied the mixture. "The *muti* must be buried right away, or it will do no good. You will know where to bury the bundle once you get there. Amai Vedu will guide you."

Tururu wrapped the bandage back around her arm and then stopped. "What about *tokoloshi*?"

"The potion will protect you. There is one more thing. On your way back, you must bury my amulet in the temple—just until the *ngozi* have had their way with Karari. I am not strong enough to resist him if he returns for it." She slid the hide band of her amulet around his neck. "Now go, before it is too late."

Tururu took the amulet and, gathering up all his courage, headed out the door with one last glance back at his grandmother.

———

Night had spread its blanket over everything by the time Tururu returned to missi's house. He peered around the storeroom wall. The light above the back step was on, as well as one in the house. He couldn't tell whether it was the one in missi's bedroom or the one in the lounge. He listened. Nothing but the sound of crickets. A half moon scarred the sky.

He glanced around the backyard. Grandmother said he would know where to bury the remedy, but he didn't have any idea where it should go. He asked Amai Vedu for guidance. Maybe by the avocado tree? It was a protected spot, and the roots had power. They would lend their force to the potion.

He started in that direction but then stopped, his attention caught by something glowing in the ground to the left of where missi had planted her sweet pea seeds. This was the area where she had built those little mud houses for her fairies. White *tokoloshi*, creatures who were good and kind. That is where he would bury the potion. Guided by the glow, he crept forward and began to dig.

He stopped. Someone was watching him. He dropped to the ground and glanced around, then looked up.

Missi! High above him floated Elizabeth, or rather a misty image of her, like one of his dead ancestors who sometimes attended Anesu's ceremonies. She stared down at him with a bewildered expression, but then recognition dawned and she smiled.

He gestured down at the spot he'd decided upon and gave her a questioning look.

She peered down, nodded, and then she was gone.

Amai Vedu! Missi was full of surprises. Bending back to his task, he dug in earth still damp from the last downpour. The soil grew warm beneath his fingers, as if it had been simmering in his mother's *sadza* pot. Another sign.

Six inches down, he dropped the clothbound *muti* into the dirt. The earth seemed to swallow it whole, collapsing over the bundle as if aiding him. He tamped down the soil, roughed it up a little, and then sat back on his heels. Closing his eyes, he chanted the words Grandmother had given him. He glanced around.

The air seemed stiller than before, yet more alive. A breeze arose, rustled through the sisal plants, the leaves of the avocado tree, and then wrapped around him in an embrace. Amai Vedu giving her approval. He'd done it. In just a little while the remedy would restore Missi back to health.

He started to rise, then stopped. She would be cured, but not safe from Karari. He groaned. Why hadn't he asked Grandmother to make a protection *muti* for missi as well?

No, he'd been lucky she'd made *this* one.

He rose to his feet. Grandmother's amulet banged against his chest, and he glanced down at it. She'd told him to bury it in the temple, but instead, he would give it to missi. It was the best protection against Karari.

He headed for the house.

Chapter 12

ELIZABETH CAME TO, FLOATING AGAINST THE CEILING. She looked down at her body sprawled on the bed, legs twisted in the sheets. Was she dead? She didn't feel dead.

She heard her mother crying, and then she was hovering above her parents in the hallway. They were headed toward her bedroom.

"You've got to let her rest," her father said in a low voice. "Remember what Doc said. She'll come through. Have faith."

"I'm telling you, she's dying," her mother said in a choked voice.

"Mom! Dad! I'm right here!" She waved her arms. "I'm all right. See? Look. Up here."

Her mother paused for a moment but then continued down the hallway. Elizabeth drifted after them, shouting as loud as she could. Still, they didn't look up. A feeling of dread came over her. Maybe she was dead.

The sound of digging broke into her awareness. It came from the yard. She drifted outside. Someone was digging in the middle of her old fairy village. She floated above the figure. Turu! Back when the family first arrived on the plantation, he'd helped her build some of the tiny fairy houses on which she'd spent so much time, showed her how to add straw to the mud mixture to make the little huts sturdy. This was when they first became friends. As if sensing her presence, he glanced up and his eyes widened.

He could see her! She wasn't dead after all.

Grabbing a bundle next to him, Turu lifted it up and gestured down at the hole with a questioning expression on his face.

She nodded. Yes. She didn't know how she knew, but that was exactly where he needed to bury the object.

"Bitty!"

Her mother's voice. She had to go. She hung there for a moment more, and then with a whoosh she was slammed back into her body. Gasping, she opened her eyes. Her mother was gripping her hand. Squinting against the light, she tried to take a breath. Her throat felt so parched.

"Oh, thank God," her mother cried. "Mac! Come quickly."

"Water."

"Here, baby. Mommy has lots of water for you."

Her head was lifted and a glass brought to her lips. She drank with loud, thirsty gulps. Water dribbled down her chin and neck. She fell back. She felt so tired, so very tired.

Elizabeth finally awoke the following evening. Her right ear ached from lying on one side for too long. Rolling over onto her back, she yawned and stretched, enjoying the pull of muscles that felt as if they'd been crammed into a matchbox for days.

Her stomach growled, which also felt good. Soft shadows played through the mosquito net draped around her bed, and the sweet smell of frangipani drifted in through the open window. Fighting dizziness, she eased up and sat against the headboard. Her head throbbed.

The door opened, and her mother appeared. "I thought I heard you." Hurrying over to the bed, she gathered up the mosquito net and tied it into a knot as high as she could reach.

Elizabeth struggled to clear the fog from her brain. "What time is it, anyway?"

Her mother pressed her palm against Elizabeth's forehead. "How do you feel?"

"Hungry. And so very thirsty."

"That's a good sign. Doc said plenty of liquids." She handed Elizabeth a glass of water. "I made you some nice soup. I'll have Chipo warm it."

"Chipo?"

"Come on, drink up," her mother said. Then she called, "Chipo! Warm *picannin dona's* soup and bring it in here, please."

Elizabeth drained the glass and wiped her mouth on her pajama sleeve. "What happened? Why's Chipo here?"

Perching on the edge of the chair beside the bed, her mother leaned forward and lifted strands of hair from Elizabeth's cheek to tuck them behind her ear. "First things first. You were poisoned and could've died. But lucky for us, you ended up vomiting. Doc thinks that's what saved you. For a while there we thought you weren't going to make it." Her voice cracked and she looked down.

Images flashed through Elizabeth's mind: floating above her parents trying to convince them she was alive, Turu digging in the yard.

"Poisoned?"

Her mother cleared her throat and looked up. "It was in the bread."

Elizabeth shook her head in confusion.

"They were trying to kill us all."

"Who?"

"Well, at first we thought it was Nelson. He was the one who made the bread, after all. But then we discovered that everything in the storeroom had been poisoned. All of it. The thing is, how on earth did anyone get in there? You know how vigilant your father is. Anyway, Mr. Bradley telephoned Gwelo to see if the main stock had been poisoned. It hadn't. So the only one who could've done it was Turu. He's the only one small enough to crawl through that little window in the storeroom."

"But—"

"Your precious Tururu. Well, let me just tell you—"

"He wouldn't. He's not like that."

"Oh yes, he most certainly is. Him and his people." Her mother's eyes glinted. "They timed it very well. The day before the official Federation holiday, and on the day everyone gets their share from the storeroom. If you hadn't eaten that piece of bread, well, all of us could've died."

"So where is Nelson now?"

"He charged off."

"And Turu?"

"He's missing as well. They're both probably with the rest of the bloody rebels."

"But, honestly, Mom. Turu would never do anything like that. I *know* him."

"So why was he in here on your bed? Pouring his vile black poison down your throat?"

Jumbled images of Turu strafed through Elizabeth's mind, the way he grabbed her after she ate the bread. He'd said something to her, what was it?

"Just because you two played together doesn't mean he has any loyalty to you." Her mother was still talking. "All this time, he's just been taking advantage of you. Using you to get out of work. You, my girl, are loyal to a fault."

"But I know he's not like that," Elizabeth said. "I mean, if I was already poisoned why would he—"

"He wanted to make sure. I mean, the piece you ate wasn't very big . . . I don't know. Honestly, who knows what goes on in their minds? When are you going to get it through your head they're not like us?"

There was a rap at the door. "Medem?"

"Come," her mother said.

Chipo appeared, balancing a tray containing a bowl of barley soup, water crackers, a glass of water, and a folded napkin. He wore Nelson's old white uniform jacket, the sleeves rolled up in order to fit. Keeping his eyes averted, he crept into the room.

"Thank you, Chipo." Her mother took the tray from him.

"Yes, medem." He turned and left the room, but not before Elizabeth caught him staring at her with a look of curiosity, like he didn't know what to make of her.

She hugged herself. Had he also been part of the plot to kill them?

"What's wrong?" Her mother shook out the napkin, tucked it beneath Elizabeth's chin, and sat back down.

"I thought Mrs. Bradley didn't trust Chipo. So why's he here?"

Her mother rolled her eyes. "That woman doesn't trust anyone. Come on, eat up."

Elizabeth ate slowly, staring down at her bowl. She took a bite of one of the water crackers. What was it Turu said to her? And then she remembered.

Missi will die.

She gasped and dropped the biscuit.

Her mother sprang to her feet. "What's the matter?"

"Uh, I just choked on the biscuit," Elizabeth said, taking a drink of water. Why would he say something like that if he . . . ?

She tried to block out the thought that he could actually have wanted to harm her.

But she couldn't. Was her mother right? Was her loyalty blocking common sense?

She fingered a scar on her chin where she'd been bitten by a stray dog when she was seven. She'd been smuggling food to the dog for days when she bent close to nuzzle him, and he snapped at her and bit her. It had meant six weeks of painful rabies injections in her stomach.

"Now there's a *munt* who's not going to give us any trouble," her mother said, lighting a cigarette.

"Who?"

"Well, Chipo, of course. Mr. Bradley knows how to keep them in line." Her mother leaned back and blew out a plume of smoke. "They respect that, you know. We've been too soft—and look where it got us."

"Chipo's going to work for us now?" Elizabeth laid down her spoon. She wasn't hungry anymore.

"We're just borrowing him until I can find another boy, what with all this going on." She leaned forward and nudged Elizabeth to eat. "Mr. Bradley got old Lindani back from the *kraal* to fill in there for now."

"There's my girl!" Elizabeth's father strode into the room, sat down on the bed beside her, and patted her leg. "How are you feeling?"

Her mother rose to her feet and headed for the door. "I'm going to see to dinner."

Elizabeth waited until she was gone and then whispered, "Is Mom right about Turu being the one who poisoned me and everything?"

"I don't know, baby. I wish I had answers for you, but I don't. Whoever actually planted the poison, Commissioner Campbell is convinced this was a plot to kill all of us in the valley. That I believe. As for Tururu, I didn't think he had it in him. Nelson perhaps, but not Tururu. But the fact of the matter is he was caught feeding you something, wasn't he? So . . . I don't know, Bitty."

Elizabeth suddenly felt exhausted. She lifted her tray, handed it to her father, and let her head flop back against the headboard. He placed the tray on the side table, then settled down beside her. She leaned her head against his shoulder and felt the prickle of tears.

"I thought he was my friend."

He kissed the top of her head. "I don't want you thinking about this anymore. You've been through a terrible ordeal, so you need as much rest as you can get. I want my little pearl to get better, all right?"

Murmuring agreement, she snuggled against him and closed her eyes, certain that she would never get back to sleep. Never, not in . . .

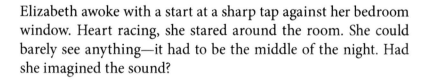

Elizabeth awoke with a start at a sharp tap against her bedroom window. Heart racing, she stared around the room. She could barely see anything—it had to be the middle of the night. Had she imagined the sound?

No. There it was again. A sharp tink against her window. She squinted toward the closed curtains. The glow from the front porch light revealed a shadow right outside her window. She shrank back.

"Missi," a loud whisper, through the half-open window.

She sat up. "Turu?"

"Please, missi."

Heart thudding, she elbowed the mosquito net out of the way and rose from her bed. The room spun. Holding onto the bed and then the chair, she stumbled over to the window. There was another clink against the glass, this one a little harder. Glancing toward her parents' bedroom across the hallway, she cracked the floor-length curtains and peered out.

Turu stood on the front lawn, shoulders hunched, his hands thrust deep into the pockets of his shorts, shifting from foot to foot. He looked more unsure of himself than ever. Slipping between the curtains, she knocked on the half-open window. Turu's head shot up. Relief flooded his face.

She glared at him. "What do you want?"

"Missi all right!"

"Surprised to see me alive?"

"Yes!"

She stared at him, unsure what to make of his confession.

"Quickly, missi. Take *nadira*." He removed an amulet from around his neck.

At first she thought it was his personal amulet, but then she realized the figure looked a little larger. Gathering the amulet and cord into a pile, he held it out in his cupped hands. "Please to take."

She stared at him. What kind of trickery was this? "What am I supposed to do with that thing?"

"Grandmother's *nadira*. Big magic. Keep missi safe."

Elizabeth peered down at a hawklike soapstone creature with some kind of milky white gemstone for an eye. It looked familiar, the same shape she'd seen in a display at the ancient Zimbabwe ruins down south. Mesmerized by its strange beauty, she reached through the window. Almost tripping over his own feet in his haste, Turu pressed the amulet and cord into her palm.

She stared down at the soapstone creature. Did she imagine that or did the little bird move, like it was fluttering its wings? She lifted it up for a closer look.

"Um, missi?"

She gave a start and, looking up at him, forced a hard voice. "So why are you giving me this?"

"To protect missi from . . ." He bit his lip.

"From what?"

"Very bad *muntu*."

She stared at him. Did this mean that his gang would be back for another try? "You've got to tell me who—"

"Bitty?"

She whipped around, becoming tangled in the curtains for a moment. "Dad!"

"What on earth are you doing by the window?"

"I-I thought I heard something out there, but it was nothing. Just an owl, I think." Covered by the curtain, she slipped the amulet into her pajama pocket.

"You need your rest."

"What are you doing up?"

"Your mom's having trouble sleeping again. The baby, you know."

She nodded.

"You poor girl," he said, his voice catching. In two steps he had enveloped her in a tight hug. "I'm so sorry you had to go through all this. I should've done a better job of protecting you."

Melting into his hug, Elizabeth could feel the amulet press against her chest. Why had she lied to him? Was she being too trusting again?

But the amulet felt warm and comforting. She felt safe with it in her pocket.

Three days later, her baby brother was born. James Archibald McKenzie. He was seven weeks early. They said it was all the excitement over Elizabeth's poisoning. She finally had a permanent live-in friend.

Chapter 13

I T HAD BEEN A MONTH SINCE TURURU GAVE ELIZABETH HIS grandmother's amulet. Since then, he had spent the long days and nights hiding away in her hut and remembering all the humiliations he'd suffered at the hands of the whites. All those times he'd been accused of lying and stealing. All those times they'd spoken to him like he was too stupid to understand.

Even Missi Elizabeth. The way she looked at him when he gave her the amulet. The most sacred possession of his people— magic, something to be honored. Instead she'd looked at it like it was some dirty old piece of rubbish. And after he'd disobeyed his grandmother to give it to her!

Medem and, no doubt, the bwana wanted to kill him, which meant he couldn't collect the rations he and Grandmother now desperately needed. Worst of all, the BSAP were after him. He found this out from his mother the night after he'd sneaked over to the *kraal* to check on her.

She also told him that his father and four other villagers had been rounded up that very day. As far as he knew, his father was now in jail. From the looks of things, that's where he would stay. He'd also learned with relief that Karari and Tutenda had headed south, Karari boasting that he was going to join the leaders of the revolution.

Now, as Tururu stood beside his grandmother in the shade of the old thorn tree by the well, he watched Mutembi, a sisal worker from the village, head home with one of her love potions in his pocket. The villagers, scared off for a while after Karari's attack, had started trickling back.

Tururu glanced down at his grandmother, at her labored movements as she collected her magic bones, the way she held her bad hand, its bandage always pulsing with an unhealthy blue glow. Good thing she kept it hidden from her customers.

Was she healing? Or was he fooling himself?

"I told you they would return," Grandmother said. "Thanks be to Amai Vedu."

Tururu glanced hungrily at the live, trussed-up chicken Mutembi had left in payment. It had been a while since they had fresh meat. His mother sometimes brought *mealies* from her garden, but since his father's arrest she too was struggling.

He lifted the chicken by the rope, binding it. "Tururu cooks the chicken now?"

Grandmother held out her arm for his help. "First we will honor Jasu. Then your lesson. And then, yes, we will eat."

Sighing, Tururu freed the bird, which made a mad dash across the dirt toward the well and began to peck at something only it could see. Their old goat turned, stared at it for a moment, and then moved to the other side of the well. The chicken would stay in the yard. None of the animals ever left Grandmother's compound; her magic saw to that. With one last hungry look at the bird, Tururu followed Grandmother into the hut.

He helped her prepare everything they would need for the ritual, then stood beside her while she lit a candle made of pork fat and dried bembi—a plant with small yellow flowers, like the sun, for Jasu, God of the Sun. Then she poured specially prepared oil on the ground in the center of her hut as an offering to Gurutu, Goddess of the Underworld. Finally, she scattered a special mix of herbs and powders to the wind for Mwari, God of the Ancestors.

As Tururu watched her, he thought of how, on this new moon, she'd been unable to make the journey to the temple to cast her special magic to rid the valley of the whites. Not so long ago, he would've been glad of that. Now he wasn't so sure.

What if Karari had been right—that Grandmother's plan was too slow? What would the leaders do to change things?

This was the first time he'd given much thought to the ones they called the leaders. He didn't even know any of their names, except for the one they called Dr. Banda. All he knew about him was that he was in neighboring Nyasaland, now part of the new Federation, and fighting to make whites give them more say in the government.

"Sabata?"

He glanced over at his grandmother. She motioned him over to her worktable, where she had managed to climb onto her stool.

"Grandmother, are you not too tired?"

"Sabata thinks he can miss a lesson today, of all days, eh?"

For the next hour he sat beside her, reciting ingredients for various cures. Then he mixed a potion like the one she'd mixed for Mutembi. She congratulated him, told him he was coming along nicely. He beamed.

Later, as he was cleaning up, he realized she had become very quiet. He glanced over at her. She was staring out the door, a strange look on her face.

"What is it, Grandmother?"

She took a deep breath. "You must leave this place. There is no future for you here. The BSAP will eventually catch you. And ever since your father disappeared, you have been without the guidance of the man spirit. Even though he is a stupid man, he is Shona and wise to the duties of Shona men. But I doubt he will return, and Sabata must go through the ritual of manhood with the guidance of a man. A man must also finish the last of *godobori* training for the man-child chosen by Amai Vedu. That is why I have decided that you must go to your uncle."

He gaped at her. "Uncle Leffy?"

His uncle had stormed out of their lives when Grandmother chose Karari as her successor instead of him, her own son. He refused to accept Amai Vedu's decree that he should become a teacher. Tururu had been a small child when his uncle left. All he remembered of him was his size—in Tururu's memory, as tall as a black monkey thorn tree—and his sternness.

"After the full moon of Chibumbi, you will go to him. He does not expect you. But he will do his duty. He is Shona, and he is destined to teach."

"But what about Grandmother?"

"What about Grandmother?"

He bit his lip. He didn't want to say the words. *Grandmother is sick.*

"Anesu is a *godobori*. All goes according to Amai Vedu's plan. If I am weak, it is because it is Amai Vedu's will. And now it is her will that you go to Leffy." She patted him on the shoulder. "Grandmother will miss Sabata."

Tururu stared down at his hands. He was filled with sadness and fear, but there was also a nub of excitement inside him at the prospect of the future he now faced. At the back of his mind, thoughts of Elizabeth arose. He would never again see her, and that brought conflicting feelings as well.

"Come, Sabata, help Grandmother up to throw the bones."

He helped Grandmother outside to her stool. She plopped down, a look of grim determination on her face, and tucked her great skirts between her knees. Propping the elbow of her bandaged hand on one knee, she snatched up the bones with her good hand and shook them next to her ear. A quick muttered prayer to Amai Vedu, and the bones flew from her fingers onto the ground.

She leaned forward. Her good eye darted over the assortment of animal bones. She turned her head this way and that, like she did every other time she'd tried to read them.

Tururu sat in the dirt beside her stool, hugging his knees and staring down at the bones. Would she be able to see clearly this time? Ever since Karari had turned the *ngozi* on her, seeing into the bones had been hit or miss. When she was able to see anything, the images were mostly blurry. But between the bones and news from the villagers, they at least had an idea what Karari was up to.

One thing they learned was that he had embarrassed the African leaders with his drunken carousing and flashy, unpredictable magic. It had only made the bwanas seem right— that the Africans were not ready for any kind of power.

Suddenly Grandmother stiffened and stared more intently at the bones.

"Grandmother?"

She continued to stare down at the bones, clucking her tongue.

Tururu glanced from Grandmother to the bones, then back again. Had she regained her sight? "What does Grandmother see?"

"Karari. I see him clearly. The *ngozi*, they are finishing him, more quickly than Anesu believed. These bad things he is doing are making them more powerful, and they are eating him from inside. He knows something bad is happening to him. He pretends it is not so. But even if he had thought it is because of the *ngozi*, he would not believe it. He thinks he is *godobori*. He thinks he is so very important. But the *ngozi* will destroy him." She stopped and frowned. "Unless . . ."

"What, Grandmother?"

"My amulet. You must fetch my amulet from the temple."

Tururu stiffened. "What? Um, why?"

"Do not worry, Grandmother will give Sabata protection from *tokoloshi*." Anesu hoisted herself up from her stool with a groan and started toward her hut. "But with all you have learned and the change I see in you, perhaps you do not need it, eh?"

"No. I mean, yes," Tururu called after her, his mind racing around like a frightened mouse looking for a hole before the hawk scooped it up. How was he going to get the amulet back from Elizabeth in time? Could he get past the BSAP, the bwana, and medem? And if he did, would Elizabeth give it back, or would she turn him in?

Chapter 14

ELIZABETH SAT CROSS-LEGGED IN HER TREE HOUSE, fanning herself with her hand. Thanks to her dad's help it had grown almost into a real room: two plywood walls and a plank floor with a trapdoor in the middle. The branches above provided an airy covering that was nearly a roof. It was midafternoon, the sun halfway down a bleached-out sky. The drone of cicadas filled the air. The hot season was almost upon them.

Her history book lay open in front of her—she had a test coming up with Mr. Coetzee in a week—but she couldn't concentrate. Her mind was on Jiminy. That's what she called her baby brother, instead of James or Jimmy. He reminded her of that little cricket from *Pinocchio*: head too large for his bird body, all that thick black hair, and when he wasn't crying or vomiting, he chirped.

He'd been born in the middle of the night and had almost died. Both he and her mother had been rushed to the hospital in Gwelo after Doc Goodwin had done everything he could in the house. And that's where they stayed for a week. Elizabeth and her father visited whenever they could. Otherwise she went to work with him at the curing sheds or out in the fields, helping whenever he let her. Ever since her mother and Jiminy had come home, her mother shuffled around in her dressing gown and looked like a smudge-eyed ghost. No one got much sleep.

All Jiminy did was cry and vomit, and his little tadpole body was always covered in some kind of rash—Mrs. Coetzee had knitted him tiny mittens so he wouldn't scratch himself. Her mother didn't have enough of her own milk, so they had to feed him cow's milk. But worst of all, his heart was too big and it didn't work properly.

Elizabeth had learned most of this from overhearing it. No one told her anything. It was like she didn't exist until she made a noise, and then her name was mud. She wanted so badly to help take care of Jiminy, but she wasn't allowed near him. To hear her mother tell it, she could kill him with all the germs she was carrying. Even her father had no time for her, what with the harvesting season and Bradley's plan to convert some of his land to tobacco. And with Turu gone, she didn't even have anyone to talk to or play with.

She had never felt so alone in her life.

From the corner of her eye, she saw Chipo heading toward the clothesline. He was lugging a tubful of diapers and some of the jackets and booties her mother had started knitting the moment she discovered she was pregnant. All blue. How sure her mother had been of a boy.

Chipo was now theirs. Forever. Mrs. Bradley had found another houseboy. Elizabeth kept an eye on him at all times, though she couldn't quite put her finger on why she didn't trust him. At least Nelson had showed how he felt about her. She didn't even hassle Chipo like she had Nelson; he mostly ignored her, especially when her parents were out of sight.

From down the road, a cloud of dust turned into the family Ford: her parents and Jiminy returning from yet another visit to Doc Goodwin. Maybe this time there would be good news. Maybe things were finally turning around. They just had to.

By the time she climbed down the tree, her mother and Jiminy were in the house and her father was headed back down the driveway toward the curing sheds. She waved at him, then rushed into the house, burst into her parents' bedroom, and collided with her mother, who was tiptoeing out of the room. They cracked heads.

"Ouch!" Elizabeth cried.

Jiminy wailed.

"Dammit, Elizabeth! He was sleeping."

"Sorry, Mom."

Avoiding her mother's glare, Elizabeth rubbed her head and glanced over at her brother's spidery arms flailing in the air. His wailing grew louder and had a raw-throated intensity Elizabeth recognized. He was hungry. Starving.

Her mother grabbed the hair on both sides of her head as if she was going to tear it out. "I can't take it. I just can't take it anymore!"

"Mommy?"

Jiminy continued to wail. Elizabeth's head rang.

"I finally got him to sleep in the car, and now you just went and woke him up."

"I'm sorry. I-I, didn't mean to." Elizabeth felt the tears well up. "I was just so glad you finally came home. Is he better?"

Her mother stared at her. The anger in her eyes drained away, replaced by tears. She fell back against the wall and stared up at the ceiling as if for an answer, then straightened and gathered Elizabeth into her arms. "I am so sorry, Bitty. Mommy's just so tired."

They stood that way for a moment, accompanied by Jiminy's now-shuddering sobs.

"Mommy really needs for you to be quiet until he gets better, all right?"

"I'm trying," Elizabeth said into her mother's chest. "I'm trying to be extra careful, honestly."

"I know." Her mother patted her on the back. "I know."

Elizabeth heard that edge she'd come to recognize creep into her mother's voice. She pulled back and looked pleadingly at her mother. "I could help you. I could change his diaper, I could help you bathe him, and I could also push him around in his pram. In the yard, or even in the house. That might make him sleep."

Jiminy continued to wail.

Her mother glanced anxiously in his direction. "Not now, all right? You just have to be patient."

But she had been patient. She bit her tongue at the look of exhausted impatience that flashed across her mother's face when she didn't answer right away. She nodded quickly.

Her mother pasted on a smile. "Well, all right then. Are you ready for your history test?"

Elizabeth gave a slight shrug. "Almost."

"Good girl. Well, you'd better be off then and get busy, hey?" Her mother turned back toward the crib.

Elizabeth headed toward the tree house. As she passed the portable radio in the kitchen, tuned to Johannesburg's Springbok Radio, it burst to life. "Dr. Kamazu Banda of Nyasaland had this to say: 'You cannot bring to Central Africa partnership by force. Partnership between the Europeans and the Africans can only come from our hearts and minds. We, the Africans of Nyasaland and Northern and Southern Rhodesia, are people. Human beings. We will continue to fight . . .'"

Elizabeth stopped and stared at the radio. They hadn't *continued* to fight. They hadn't even *started* to fight. There hadn't been any big riots or any of the horrible acts everyone thought the natives would commit—except for those couple of incidents in Nyanga, and, closer to home, a car was stoned when a woman and her daughter hit a *picannin* on a bicycle on their way to Bulawayo. But even that had been before Federation.

After Elizabeth's poisoning, some of the white men in the valley had started carrying guns, and the BSAP came out in force. They were everywhere, day and night, stopping African boys and men on the roads and in towns, sometimes for no reason at all. They even patrolled the villages—something they didn't normally do. To put the fear of God into any *kaffir* who even fancied the idea of making trouble is what they said.

That's how Nelson got caught two days after the poisoning. He'd been rounded up with a group of "suspicious-looking *kaffirs*" at the *kraal*. And now he was in jail, swearing his innocence and keeping silent about Turu.

Turu.

Elizabeth had tried to block him from her mind. Whenever she listened to what her mother had to say about it all, she felt like a fool for trusting him.

And then there was what Mr. Coetzee and everybody else had to say about Africans in general. They were different from whites because they came from different stock. They just didn't have it in them to feel and care about things like whites did. They'd turn on you soon as look at you.

But according to her dad, people were people. We all come from the same clay. God's creations, every single one of us, he said.

All these conflicting views made her head hurt. All she knew was she couldn't shake the feeling that Turu was her friend, whatever stock he came from.

She wasn't sure about the amulet, though. That well-worn piece of soapstone he'd given her made her have a funny feeling, especially when she remembered Turu's stories of how witch doctors would sometimes turn people into zombielike creatures who would then go on to do their bidding. Yet she couldn't bring herself to chuck the amulet or smash it to pieces; for one thing, it looked really old. She thought maybe it was a relic from the people who lived in the Zimbabwe ruins. And for another, despite her fears, the little stone bird continued to feel friendly and comforting.

So she stashed it in the old cigar box Mr. Bradley had given her, where she kept all her scavenged bits of glass, scraps of paper, and holy cards for the "secrets" game she and Turu used to play. As an afterthought, she added the crucifix Sister Marcella gave her at the St. Justin Martyr School in Johannesburg. Just in case. She stowed the box in the back of her wardrobe, where she'd also tossed her old book of fairy lore.

Now she headed out the back door and stared out at the yard. It looked like she felt: prickly and glum. Her gaze landed on her sweet pea bed; tiny shoots poked up through the soil. And then she remembered Pookie pecking at the seeds.

Pookie. Her only friend. And now he was dead. She sank to the ground. Tears rose, and in moments she was sobbing.

That night Elizabeth lay in bed trying to ignore Jiminy's cries and her mother's attempts to soothe him to sleep. He kept making these ack-ack sounds that weren't really crying. More like he didn't have enough strength to cry. The sound cut right through Elizabeth. She pulled the pillow over her head, but she could still hear him.

Earlier she'd heard her parents talking about their visit to Doc Goodwin. Her mother was going to have to start feeding Jiminy a special formula because it looked like he was allergic to cow's milk. And then they spoke of Doc's findings—some kind of test—that said Jiminy was "slow." What they meant was that he was retarded.

Elizabeth had known a retarded girl at St. Justin Martyr. Her name was Agatha. She was older and bigger than everyone else—and round, with thick black eyebrows and a permanent smile. All Agatha wanted was to be friends with everybody. She made Elizabeth feel dreadful, torn between wanting to befriend her and afraid it might make her look like a fool in front of her friends. All the other children were horrible to her. And when they weren't being horrible they just ignored her, which was horrible in a different way.

And now that's what was going to happen to her little brother. That's if he didn't die first. She couldn't let that happen. She had to do something to make him better. She didn't know exactly what, but she knew she couldn't just wait around.

If only Turu were here. He could get his grandmother to concoct some *muti* for Jiminy that would cure him. But Turu wasn't there, and she didn't know where he was. She would probably never see him again.

Suddenly she sat up. She had the amulet. It was magic. Surely, it would do the job. Or did it only work for Africans? Dare she risk seeing what it could do?

She felt her way across the darkened room to her wardrobe. It took a while of patting around in the dark to find the cigar box. Gagging any thoughts of the amulet's zombie-making power, she sat cross-legged on the floor, opened the box, and felt around for the crucifix.

She gripped that in her left hand and, with her heart threatening to burst from her chest, she clasped the amulet in her right hand. Should she just make a wish, like she did when it was a monkey's wedding? Or should she make it a proper prayer? She didn't know. But she daren't waste any more time.

She closed her eyes. Here goes.

"Please, dear amulet, and people of um, old Zimbabwe . . . Anesu . . . God of Africans . . . please make my brother better . . . all of him . . . forever and ever." She opened her eyes. Was that enough?

She closed her eyes again. "Thank you. Amen."

The amulet grew warm and seemed to swell in her hand. She almost dropped it. Was that a sign? Or was it taking her over?

She quickly stuffed it back into the cigar box, threw the crucifix in after it, closed the lid, and slid the box back into the wardrobe. She returned to her bed, where she tossed and turned all night filled with excitement, fear, and anticipation.

For the next week, Elizabeth watched and listened for signs that Jiminy was getting better. Instead, he seemed to be getting worse. His rash was back with a vengeance—he looked like a scabby little strawberry. And the formula had also started to make him vomit. Doc was looking into getting him another kind that they were going to have to fetch from Salisbury.

Doc's wife spent a couple of days with them so her mother could get some sleep. Her father was holding down the fort for Bradley while he was in Salisbury exploring his options for growing tobacco, so he was hardly around to help.

Elizabeth watched Jiminy's decline with a sinking heart. She had made him worse with her wish. She must not have done it right. The only person who knew how to work an amulet properly was a witch doctor. And the only one she knew of was Anesu. But how could she trust the old lady after her people had tried to kill her?

She spent more and more time in her tree house. That's how she saw her mother the following day, dressed in one of her old sleeveless dresses, striding through the sisal in the scorching heat. Her mother hated the sun beating down on her, she always wore a hat. But there she was, hatless, hair flying.

Back in the house, Jiminy was screaming.

Where was she going? Had something happened to Jiminy?

Elizabeth scrambled down the tree, ran into the house past Chipo washing dishes at the sink, and charged into her parents' bedroom. She leaned over the crib. Arms and legs flailing, Jiminy kept screaming, his face scarlet. Was he all right? She couldn't tell.

She ran back outside and charged toward the field. Her mother was coming back down the path toward her. She walked slowly, her head down.

"Mommy?"

Her mother stopped and lifted her head. She stared at Elizabeth as if she didn't recognize her.

"What's wrong?" Elizabeth asked. "Where did you go?"

"Uh. A walk. I just went for a little walk."

"But your hat . . . Jiminy . . . "

For a moment it seemed her mother's face might crumble, but then she drew herself up and pasted on a barely discernible smile. "I'm back now. Let's go have our tea, shall we?"

Elizabeth couldn't wait for her father to come home so she could tell him what had happened.

When she did, he looked shaken but quickly recovered. "Mommy's just having an awful time of it right now. Don't worry. It's going to be all right. Daddy will take care of everything."

Elizabeth wanted to believe him, but she was worried. Everything seemed so hopeless. They couldn't go on like this.

That night, Jiminy had another one of his crying jags. This one seemed to go on forever.

She had to do something. She was going to have to find Anesu herself. She would take the amulet with her—maybe it would help her find Anesu's hut.

She fell asleep filled with visions of a normal Jiminy, apple-cheeked and gurgling.

Chapter 15

THE NEXT DAY, ELIZABETH WAITED FOR HER CHANCE. Just after lunch, everything fell into place. As if it were meant to be.

Her father had returned to work after lunch and wouldn't be home until at least five o'clock. Jiminy was finally asleep, which meant her mother was also asleep. With Jiminy quiet, she would almost certainly stay that way. Even Chipo had the afternoon off, so she didn't have to worry about him telling on her.

With Jiminy's hooded pram parked next to the back step, one of his baby bottles filled with water tucked in beside the mattress, and Anesu's amulet around her neck, she tiptoed into her parents' bedroom holding Jiminy's pacifier. She'd dipped it in gripe water—a sweet, soothing *muti* he liked. Once she stuck it in his mouth, she would have to hurry because the gripe water usually gave him hiccups after a while. She wanted to be far away from the house by then.

The bedroom curtains were drawn, as usual. Her mother lay on the far side on the bed, facing the opposite wall. She made small snoring sounds. A good sign.

Elizabeth tiptoed toward the crib and peered down at her brother. Mingled odors of baby powder, milk, and vomit filled her nostrils. Dressed in an undershirt and diaper, he lay on his back, his chamomile-covered body making him look like a miniature war-painted African warrior. He had the longest eyelashes she'd ever seen.

He stirred, jerked, and blinked up at her.

"Jiminy, Timiny," she whispered.

His face screwed up and he opened his mouth to cry. She shoved in the pacifier, slipped her arms beneath him, and lifted him from the crib, almost hitting his head on the side. Eyes wide and glistening with tears, he reached up, grabbed a strand of her hair, and tried to pull himself up.

She bit her lip against the pain and hurried from the room. He made small sucking sounds on his pacifier as she half ran through the kitchen and down the back steps.

She lowered him into his pram, all the while trying to keep him in the shade because of his allergic reaction to direct sunlight. The amulet fell from her blouse and dangled over his face.

He let go of her hair and tried to grab it.

"You like that, don't you?" She removed the amulet from her neck and slipped it over his head.

He stared cross-eyed down at it lying on his chest and waved his arms, trying to reach it. She slipped into her sandals, grasped the pram handle, and headed across the backyard past Chipo's room.

The sound of BBC news, drifting in and out from the radio in the kitchen, followed them: "Entertainment news. *From Here to Eternity* won the Oscar . . . minor acts of civil disobedience . . . trade unionist Joshua Nkomo and his followers continue in the larger cities. They want an audience with Prime Minister Sir Godfrey Huggins."

She stopped. What if she couldn't find Anesu's hut? What if her mother awoke? What if someone came over for a visit?

She shook herself. She couldn't think that way. She *had* to do this.

She plunged ahead, past the blue gum trees and onto the well-worn path. The wheels slipped smoothly along the ruts as she hurried along, accompanied by the thrum of cicadas and a small cloud of flies. No sound came from the pram. She squinted up at the sun. It was hotter than she'd counted on.

Once past the ruins, she stopped and peered in at her brother. He'd fallen asleep, the pacifier dangling from the corner of his mouth. Sweat made faint trails down his chamomile-covered face. She waved away a fly perched on his nose, straightened, and looked around.

Van Zyl's shop lay directly ahead, and somewhere to her left, just beyond that distant rise, lay Anesu's hut. She didn't know exactly where, but she had an idea of what it looked like.

She gazed at the expanse of dry scrub stretching for miles, then took a deep breath and started across the uneven ground. The pram rocked and bounced, tossing Jiminy around. He began to cry. She stopped and stuck the bottle of water in his mouth. He sucked thirstily for a moment, then spat out the teat and cried again.

"Okay, listen. In just a little while we're going to find the nice witch doctor and she's going to make Jiminy Timiny all better. All right?"

He wailed, arched his back, and thrashed this way and that.

Gripping the pram handle as tight as she could to hold it steady, she continued toward the hillock. Jiminy's crying turned into a kind of moaning. Sweat began to seep into her eyes. She knew she should've taken a sip of Jiminy's water, but she didn't want to stop.

That rise was farther away than she'd thought. Her arms ached, and a blister was forming on her heel. Jiminy's moaning was all but drowned out by the pram's rattling.

She finally reached the rise and ploughed up to the top. Gasping for breath, she stopped and stared down the other side.

No hut.

She groaned. What made her think she knew where it was? Her and her stupid ideas. She squinted up at the sun. How long had they been gone? She had never figured out how to tell time from the sun, like Turu did. What if her mother was already awake? What if her father had decided to return home early?

She was in such big trouble. She had been stark raving mad to do this.

She scanned the area in front of her one last time. That image, or feeling, or whatever it was that she'd had of Anesu's hut had been so real at the time. But where was it?

She was going to have to give up and turn back. "Sorry, Jiminy."

She turned the pram around and was about to start down the hill when she realized that the landscape back was as stark and unfamiliar as that on the other side of the rise. Where was van Zyl's shop, the baobab tree? The ruins? She should be able to see them from here. She couldn't even see her own tracks in the dirt.

They were well and truly lost. Her knees felt weak. Tears welled up. Jiminy howled.

"Ssh, it's all right," she whispered. "It's going to be all right."

He gave a dry-throated screech.

She turned and looked back toward the open veld, to where the hut should've been. There was another rise ahead. Maybe that was the one. She had to give it one more try. She brushed away her tears with both hands, turned the pram around again, and set off down the hillock at a dead clip.

Ignoring the jarring pain in her arms and shoulders and Jiminy's screaming, she kept going until she reached the top of the next knoll. Sweat blurred her vision. Her breath rasped in her throat, and her heart threatened to burst from her rib cage. Panting, she crested the rise.

No hut! She gave a wail.

And then it struck her. Jiminy had stopped crying. She snatched up the blanket. He lay on his back, arms and legs pumping, mouth stretched wide in a soundless scream. He was turning purple!

She gaped down at him for a moment, too stunned to move. "Don't die! Oh, please don't die."

She scooped him up from the pram, and in the process smacked his head against the hood. He let out a shriek and arched his back. She lost her grip, and he fell back into the pram with a thud, lay still for a moment, and then started drawing in exhausted, shuddering breaths. An angry scratch appeared above his eyebrow.

"Nooo!" She fell to her knees beside the pram.

All she'd wanted to do was help him, steer her mother clear of another nervous breakdown, and wipe that helpless look off her father's face. She'd made such a mess of things.

Jiminy whimpered. His diaper was soaked. She hadn't even thought to bring him a clean one. She groaned and reached into the pram to pat his chest. His heart. Like a caged bird beating against her hand. It couldn't take much more of this.

The amulet.

She felt around, found it, and gripped it tightly. "Please help me. I beg of you, help me and Jiminy. Just this once."

She waited a couple of moments. And then, holding her breath, she sat up and scanned the horizon.

No hut in sight.

She threw the amulet back into the pram and let her head drop back. "Arrgh!"

Above her, the leaves of a black monkey thorn tree rustled softly in the breeze.

The tree in her vision. Anesu's hut must be here!

Of course she couldn't see it. It wouldn't just be sitting out here on the veld, visible to any old body. It was a magic hut, after all. How could she make it appear? She didn't have much to go on. Just an idea and a feeling.

She rose to her feet and closed her eyes. She concentrated. But nothing came to mind. Trying not to panic, she thought and thought and thought. Still nothing. But then she dug deep inside herself and reached out to Anesu with all of her heart and all of her mind.

"I know you're here. I believe in you," she whispered. "You're the only one who can help me. Please, let me come to you." She took a deep breath and cried, "Come forth, oh great hut!"

The air stirred around her, and she opened her eyes. A short distance away, down a gentle slope, sat a hut with walls the rich color of a gazelle's hide and thatch that was plump and golden. A strange, mesmerizing, blue-tinged fire burned in front.

For a moment all she could do was stare. She'd done it.

Jiminy bleated.

She grinned down at him. "We're here, Jiminy. Everything is going to be all right now."

She grabbed the pram handle and charged down the slope. A mangy goat at the side of the hut inched around to look at them, tail twitching at the flies circling its rump.

A gaunt black woman leaning on a walking stick appeared in the hut's arched doorway. She wore a brightly colored *douk* on her head and clothes that seemed two sizes too large. She clutched a bandaged hand to her chest.

Elizabeth slowed.

Surely this couldn't be Turu's grandmother. He described her as very big, and what was that funny blue glow coming from her bandaged hand?

The old woman fixed Elizabeth with a hard stare, one of her eyes a funny milky color. Elizabeth stopped, suddenly afraid.

Jiminy whimpered, so she gathered her courage and cleared her throat. "Anesu?"

The old woman continued to stare at her.

Elizabeth shot a quick, nervous glance over her shoulder "Um, I was hoping you could help my little brother. You see, he's sick all the time. It's his heart, and he's always vomiting and crying and they think he's—"

"*Picannin dona?*"

Elizabeth nodded and eagerly and pushed the pram toward Anesu. "Yes! Yes, it's me, Elizabeth."

Anesu watched her approach, then looked down at Jiminy. Her gaze softened. But then she stiffened, reached into the pram with her good hand, and pulled out the amulet. The amulet glowed, the eye glinting as it swung back and forth.

"Where *picannin dona* get *nadira*?"

"Uh, T-turu."

Anesu's expression hardened as she stuffed the amulet into her voluminous skirt pocket. Elizabeth opened her mouth to protest but closed it again. She'd begun to believe the amulet was hers.

Anesu turned and hobbled into the hut. "Bring *picannin bwana* inside."

Swatting at flies, Elizabeth hefted Jiminy onto her hip. She grimaced as his soaked diaper seeped through her shorts. She started after Anesu. Jiminy moaned and peered at her through eyes almost swollen shut with tears. The cut above his eye was caked with blood.

The flies didn't follow them into the hut.

She trailed Anesu to a long wooden table covered with an array of old pickle, jam, and mayonnaise jars that had once occupied the McKenzie pantry shelf.

The old woman reached under the table, removed a faded blanket, and clumsily spread it on the table with her good hand. She indicated for Elizabeth to lay Jiminy down. Eyeing the various containers behind Anesu, Elizabeth hesitated.

What was in all those jars and bottles? Monkey brains, snake tongues, ground-up cockroaches? Was the old woman going to feed any of that stuff to Jiminy?

Anesu watched her from beneath hooded lids.

Elizabeth suppressed a shudder and hoisted Jiminy onto the table. He burst out crying. Anesu laid her good hand over his heart, closed her eyes, and muttered something.

Jiminy stopped crying and gazed up at her.

Anesu kept her eyes closed. She seemed to be listening. After a moment she gave a slight knowing nod, opened her eyes and, making cooing sounds, eased off Jiminy's undershirt. She tossed it onto the floor, removed his soaked diaper, and held it up in front of Elizabeth. "Do you have another?"

Elizabeth colored. "I-I forgot to bring one."

"Tsk, tsk."

Anesu dropped the diaper on the floor and bent over to inspect Jiminy. She turned him this way and that and peered into his mouth, his ears, and examined the scratch above his eyebrow.

Jiminy gurgled the whole time, just like Elizabeth dreamed he might.

Anesu indicated for Elizabeth to open a big jar of brown goo. Holding her breath in case the stuff stank, Elizabeth opened it, then stepped back. She watched Anesu slather the thick ointment all over Jiminy, turning him brown. He made faces like he might start crying again, but then he closed his eyes and lay still.

Elizabeth gasped. Oh my God, the old woman had killed him. She took a step forward, only to see his chest rise and fall. A tiny snore escaped from his parted lips.

Anesu watched him for a moment, then leaned over and scooped a ladleful of water from the pail near her feet, took a sip, and held it out to Elizabeth.

Elizabeth hesitated. She'd never taken a drink after a black person before. They weren't allowed to use the house utensils. And was the water clean? But she was parched. She took the ladle, turned it to a different spot, and after taking a test sip, downed water that was cool, and fresh, and oh-so-sweet.

She wiped her mouth with the back of her hand and dropped the ladle back into the pail. "Thank you. That was really good."

The old woman gave her the tiniest of nods. Then, holding one end of a frayed towel in her good hand and gripping the other end in her teeth, she tore it in half and slid it under Jiminy's bottom. Elizabeth reached over and helped her tie the ends into a knot.

They stood looking down at their handiwork.

Jiminy snoozed on. This was the first time Elizabeth had ever helped with his diaper, and it felt good.

Chapter 16

TURURU KNEW SOMETHING WAS DIFFERENT THE MOMENT his grandmother's hut appeared. He ran down the incline, gripping the sack of cornmeal on his head with both hands. Everything felt wrong.

Karari!

Lowering the sack to the ground, he crouched, then crept up to the hut window and peered inside. Blinded from the sun, he struggled to make out the figure standing next to his grandmother's stooped form at her worktable. Their backs were to him.

Missi? What was she doing here? How had she found Grandmother's hut?

"Sabata!"

He jumped. That tone of voice. The amulet. Grandmother had found out about the amulet! Heaving a big sigh, he rose and slunk into the hut, dropped the bag of cornmeal, and looked down at his toes.

"Didn't I tell you to bury *nadira*?"

Tururu sneaked a glance at missi. She lifted her fingers in greeting. He scowled at her.

"Well?" Grandmother said.

He lifted one shoulder. "Sabata wanted to protect missi from Karari."

"You disobeyed me and you lied."

"Sabata's very sorry . . ."

Grandmother considered him for a moment. "How did the white girl find my hut?"

He shrugged. That's what he wanted to know too.

A fluttery movement to the left of his grandmother caught his eye. A small, brown-skinned baby lay on the table, a very small creature with one of Grandmother's old towels wrapped around its bottom. The creature was sound asleep. "Who is *bebe*?"

Grandmother inclined her head toward Elizabeth. "Missus's brother."

"But he is brown."

"Anesu's *muti*. She brought him here for my help."

He had two thoughts. From the looks of the *picannin* bwana, he would fit inside the little car Tururu had built for him. But what astonished Tururu—and also hurt him—was the fact that Grandmother was helping missi. Why? She hated whites.

Grandmother turned to Elizabeth. "Missus, you tell Anesu. How did you find my hut?"

"I'm not sure. I knew it was over here . . . somewhere. But I couldn't find it, so I . . . well, I just . . ." She suddenly felt embarrassed at the rawness of the feelings she'd experienced reaching out to Anesu on the ridge. "I sort of just *felt* you were here. So I just asked for you to let me come to you, then I looked up and there you were."

The old woman gazed at her for a long moment, nodded, and placed her good hand on top of Elizabeth's head. Elizabeth gave a start, but then she stood still.

Finally, Grandmother looked up with a frown. Shaking her head, she looked at Elizabeth with grudging respect, removed the amulet from her pocket, and slid it back over Elizabeth's head.

Tururu gaped. She was giving a white person her precious amulet. Had the ngozi poisoned her in the head?

Elizabeth lifted the amulet and gazed down at it with glowing eyes. "You've giving it to me? It's mine now?"

"No."

"But, I don't understand—"

Grandmother fixed Elizabeth with a fierce stare. "*Nadira* sacred. You take good care of *nadira*."

"Oh, I will. I promise. But—"

"*Never* give *nadira* to anyone. Do you understand Anesu?"

"Yes!"

"And remember this. *Nadira* cannot be taken."

Elizabeth opened her mouth as if to say something but then closed it again and nodded.

Grandmother stared at her for a long moment, like she was thinking a lot of things, and then bent down and retrieved a bucket behind the one filled with water. She held it out toward Tururu. "Goat's milk for *bebe*."

"Oh no," Elizabeth said. "He'll just vomit."

Tururu took the bucket and, looking from his grandmother to Elizabeth and back again, hesitated.

"Go," Grandmother said.

Tururu continued out the door and headed for the goat while Elizabeth continued to protest behind him. "You see, he's allergic to milk and formula and well, everything. He'll just vomit it all up."

As Tururu milked the goat, he found himself wishing missi hadn't come. Seeing her again after all this time, reminded him of how suspicious she had been when he gave her the amulet.

He returned with the milk and plunked the bucket on the table harder than he meant to. Milk sloshed up. The small brown creature on the other end of the table gave a short jerk of surprise and blew a spit bubble.

Elizabeth glanced anxiously at the bucket. "How long will it take for the brown to fade?"

Grandmother shrugged and reached into the bucket with a piece of cloth. She let it soak for a moment, then dribbled the milk into the *bebe's* mouth. He sucked hungrily.

"He *will* vomit. I'm telling you," Elizabeth said.

Grandmother kept feeding him in that way until he pinched his lips together and swatted away the dripping cloth. Elizabeth watched with uneasy eyes, then folded her arms. The small bwana smiled and gurgled, goat's milk staining his mouth.

Ten minutes later, Grandmother had him back in the pram, ready to go, and still no vomiting. Elizabeth continued to stare at him.

Grandmother patted her arm. "It is all right, missus, bwana will not be sick."

Elizabeth turned to her with shining eyes. "So he's all better, then?"

"Oh no, missus. Anesu cannot make *picannin* bwana *all* better."

"But I thought with that chant you did, and the *muti*—"

"He is *dofo*. That I cannot change. For Shona, children like this, they are the gods' treasures. We take care of them as they are. They teach us who *we* are."

Tururu stared down at the small brown one, who was now asleep. *Dofo.* He wondered how she could tell in someone so young.

"You mean he's always going to be . . . *dofo*?" Elizabeth asked.

Grandmother shrugged. "That is up to the gods."

Her face crumpled. Despite everything, Tururu felt sorry for her.

Grandmother patted Elizabeth's arm and handed her a tin of Zambuck ointment.

"Zambuck?" she said. "But that's for mosquito bites, and burns and things. It doesn't turn your skin brown."

"This muti Anesu make special, not the same as the one I put on bwana—that one is strong. This one very good, and it will not make bwana's skin brown."

"Oh, good. Thank you. She popped the tin into her pocket.

"And, missus, do you remember what Anesu say about *nadira*?"

"Oh yes. *Never* give *nadira* to anyone. I won't. Not ever." She slipped the amulet inside the neckline of her dress. "Thank you. Thank you so much. And now I'd really better go."

Grandmother turned to Tururu. "Take missus back."

Tururu started to say that missi could find her own way back, but Grandmother glared at him and jerked her head toward the pram. He knew better than to defy her. He stomped toward it.

Grandmother turned to Elizabeth and, with a smile, lifted her chin in good-bye.

"Bye-bye," Elizabeth said. "Thank you again."

Without waiting to see if Elizabeth was following, Tururu gripped the pram handle and set off at a fast clip across the clearing. He was halfway up the incline before he realized she wasn't behind him. He turned to see her standing in front of the fire pit, staring down at the *ngozi* flames. He could tell she was mesmerized.

"Missi!"

She continued to stare down. Yelling again, he ran back and tugged on her arm.

"They're just like little blue fairies," she whispered.

"No, missi. *Ngozi.* Bad. *Very* bad."

She turned back. "They can't be."

"Come, missi!" He steered her back toward the pram. "I tell you, they are dangerous. We must go."

Still stealing glances back at the fire, Elizabeth followed him.

Tururu steered the pram up the incline. He didn't want to have to talk to her. She trudged behind him, taking an occasional glance over her shoulder.

Keeping an eye on her, he passed the black monkey thorn tree and then started down the incline and across the veld toward the shortcut. He would be glad to see the last of missi, but he was sorry he would not be able to give the small bwana the car he'd made. He thought of asking her to retrieve it for him but changed his mind. He didn't want to have to say anything more than was necessary.

"What was that about Karari?" She came up beside him. "He's the one you said poisoned me, right?"

"Shh." He glanced around. "Do not say his name."

"Why not? You said his name earlier."

"He cannot hear or see inside Grandmother's hut. Outside is different."

She stopped, realization dawning in her eyes. "That was *him* wasn't it? That ghost I saw slipping into the storeroom? So *that's* how the poison got there."

He nodded and kept walking.

She followed. "Where is he now?"

He lifted his chin in the general direction of Bulawayo and places beyond, oddly reluctant to reveal where Karari might be: one *muntu* in trouble, all *muntu* in trouble.

"Is he coming back here?"

"Missi has *nadira*," he said in a tight voice. "Missi safe."

"Is that why she gave it back to me?"

"Only Anesu and Amai Vedu know."

"How long do you think she'll let me keep it?"

He didn't answer.

"I thought you said she really hated white people."

He had thought so too. He picked up his pace.

She caught up to him. "Turu, what happened to your grandmother's hand?"

She was like a fly buzzing around his head. He could only swat at it with answers. "*Ngozi.*"

"Those little blue fairies?" She glanced back in the direction of the hut, a look of disbelief on her face.

Tururu stopped and glanced around. With all her nattering, he'd almost passed the spot where he could cut across the veld. Elizabeth stumbled into him.

She took a couple steps back. "But how? I mean . . . ?"

Without answering her, he turned to his right and steered the pram down a path that ran through the peanut field where he'd been poisoned.

"You've never told me about this shortcut," she said.

He didn't answer.

"Hey! Why're you acting so horrible?"

He kept walking.

"You're being very rude, you know."

He glanced back but didn't stop. She stood in the middle of the path with her hands on her hips. He half expected her to run up and give him a whack on the back of his head.

He picked up his pace. A few minutes more and he'd be rid of her. As soon as he saw the roof of bwana Mac's house, he parked the pram in the middle of the path, whirled around, and, giving her a wide berth, ran back toward Grandmother's hut.

"I hate you!" she called after him.

Good.

Chapter 17

ELIZABETH WATCHED TURU'S BACK FOR A MOMENT, TRYING to think of something else to shout after him. Bloody *munt*, she thought.

But, truth was, he'd really hurt her feelings. She realized she'd had this crazy expectation that they'd just slip back into their old way of being together, like nothing had happened. Instead, he was cold and rude.

And then she remembered the pickle she was in. What if her mother had heard her shouting?

Glancing around, she shoved the pram the last hundred yards toward the gap in the hedge next to the avocado tree. Jiminy was still sleeping. She stopped at the hedge, grateful for its height and bushiness, and glanced up at the sun. It had slid down the sky quite a bit. She must've been gone, what, like for a couple of hours? More than that?

Please, oh please, let everything be as she left it.

She looked down at Jiminy. Oh no. He was still very brown, darker than Mr. Patel, the Indian owner of the material shop in Nkana.

Anesu hadn't answered her question about how long the color would last. Forever, maybe. That's why she hadn't answered.

The enormity of what lay ahead hit her and she stood there, wanting to run back to Anesu's hut. But she couldn't. She had to press ahead. She peered through the gap in the hedge, barely wide enough for the pram, and gasped.

The Ford sat in the driveway. Her father wasn't due home until after five o'clock! It couldn't be that late already. She glanced toward her parents' bedroom window. The curtains were still drawn, the yard deserted.

There was nothing else to do but plunge ahead. Taking a deep breath, she braced herself and wrestled the pram though the opening in the hedge, bringing a shower of twigs and leaves down on Jiminy. He opened his eyes and stared, cross-eyed, at a leaf on his nose.

She snatched it up, gave him a brilliant smile, and patted him on the tummy. "There you are, my little Jiminy Timiny. All better, hmm?" she whispered. "Please don't cry, all right?"

He obliged, all the way to the back step. She lifted him out and carried him into the kitchen. An ominous silence greeted her. Jiminy reached up, grabbed a hank of her hair, and tried to shove it into his mouth.

Eyes watering, she ran from room to room and then on into her parents' bedroom. "Mom? Dad?" she called out in a small voice.

No answer. Where were they? A terrifying thought hit her.

The rebels kidnapped them. They'd forced her father to drive over here with an assegai pressed against his throat, grabbed her mother, and then . . .

She glanced around. No blood. No signs of a struggle. Still. After all she'd experienced today, anything seemed possible. The sudden appearance of the hut, those blue fairies. And Karari.

Karari! That was it.

He'd heard her mention his name. He and his cohorts had probably rounded up all the whites in the valley with some kind of magic. She and Jiminy were the only ones left alive. They were orphans. The thought made her knees weak.

"There, there," she said to Jiminy, even though he hadn't made a peep.

Prying open his fist, she freed her hair and gently lowered him into the crib. He flailed wildly, made a prune face, and began to cry. Whipping out the amulet from her blouse, she dangled it above his head and swung it back and forth.

"Rock-a-bye baby in a tree top," she sang in a tremulous voice, "when the wind blows the cradle will rock, when the bough breaks the cradle will fall, and . . ."

She tailed off as his eyes closed, covered him with a blanket, and tiptoed over to the bed.

She fell back and stared up at the ceiling. What now? Her mind was a blank. Too much had happened.

In moments, she was sound asleep.

"Elizabeth!"

At first she thought it was a dream. But then someone shook her shoulder. She shot up, forgetting where she was for a moment. And then she remembered.

Her parents stood beside the bed, glaring at her.

"Dad! Mom! You're all right."

"Where the hell have you been?" her father asked.

She cringed at the anger in his voice. "I . . . um . . . "

"What did you do to Jimmy?" her mother cried. "Why's he brown?"

"It's—"

"I've been out of my mind with worry!"

"Have you any idea how frantic we've been?" her father asked. "We've been combing the countryside for the past hour. I was just about to fetch the BSAP."

"I was hoping to get back before you got home from work and Mom woke up and—"

"Where did you go?" her mother asked

Elizabeth stared down at her hands. She couldn't tell them she'd taken Jiminy to a witch doctor. Especially not a witch doctor who happened to be Turu's grandmother.

Her father dropped to one knee beside the bed. "You have to tell us what happened, Bitty."

"I-I just wanted to help Jiminy. He's always so sick, and Mommy was . . . Mommy was so . . . " Elizabeth began to cry. "I took him to Anesu."

"Who?" her mother asked.

"Go on," her father said.

"Anesu," Elizabeth said. "She's a witch doctor."

Her mother gasped. "You took him to a witch doctor?"

"You took Jimmy all the way to the *kraal*?" Her father's steely voice was worse than her mother's hysteria.

Elizabeth wiped away her tears. "Oh no, it wasn't *that* far away."

"Exactly where, then?"

"I don't know exactly where. I-I got all turned around, and then, and then, the hut . . . well, it just sort of appeared."

Jiminy let out a wail.

"It's all right, baby. Mommy's here now." Her mother hurried over to the crib, lifted him out, and patted him on the back. He stopped crying. "Let's get this dirty rag off you. I just hope you haven't caught some kind of nasty disease."

"So," her father said. "You were telling me . . ."

"Well . . ." Elizabeth looked back down at her hands. "I'd heard about this witch doctor, and so I went to get a cure for Jiminy."

"You just 'heard' about this witch doctor?" her father said.

"I'd heard some of the servants talking about her this one day when Turu and I went to Mr. van Zyl's for sweets." Elizabeth was amazed at the ease with which the lie rolled from her lips. "This was before Jiminy was born and—"

"Where is this hut?"

"It's sort of near Mr. van Zyl's shop."

"There's nothing between here and Mr. van Zyl's shop," her father said. "Not for miles around."

"I-I don't know. Honestly. I got terribly lost."

Her father squeezed his eyes shut and pinched the bridge of his nose between forefinger and thumb.

Her mother eased Jiminy back into his crib and slipped a pacifier into his mouth. "I'd better go and make him a bottle."

Elizabeth jumped to her feet. "Oh no! Anesu says you mustn't give him any milk."

"What?"

"Anesu says that's what makes him vomit, that you've got to give him goat's milk, like she did." Elizabeth blanched at the horrified expression on her mother's face but kept going. "She fed him over an hour ago and he hasn't vomited yet—and he's not scratching himself either. See?"

As if in answer, Jiminy gurgled.

Her mother's gaze dropped to the amulet around Elizabeth's neck. "Wait a minute, where did that thing come from?"

"I-I found it near the ruins . . . the other day."

Her mother eyed her. "When?"

"Um, a couple of weeks ago, actually."

"I've never seen you wear it before."

Her father squinted down at it. "Hmm, looks really old."

"And dirty. Get that awful thing off your neck."

"But, Mom!" Elizabeth gave her father an imploring look. "It's not dirty. It's my good luck charm. Please let me keep it."

"I said—"

"Oh, let her keep it," her father said. "It can't hurt. Besides, that's the least of our worries right now."

"Like that brown stuff all over Jimmy's body, for starters," her mother said.

Elizabeth whipped out the Zambuck tin filled with the stuff Anesu had given her, and held it up like a salesperson. "It's this *muti*—well, sort of. Only this one won't make his skin brown. But it will stop him from scratching himself."

"Zambuck?" her mother and father said together.

"That's just the tin. There's good *muti* inside. Really good. It'll fix his skin."

Her father opened the tin and smelled the contents. "Well, it's definitely not Zambuck. Smells like . . . I don't know exactly what. But not . . . awful."

Her mother peered over at the mixture. "I certainly hope his skin doesn't stay brown. What will people think?"

Elizabeth realized that her parents weren't yelling at her anymore. They were almost even listening. "Please, just give it a try." Elizabeth looked from one to the other. "You'll see. And you could probably get milk from Mr. Osborne, he's got all those goats—"

"Whoa," her father said. "You're not out of the woods yet, my girl. I'm really disappointed in you. I thought you knew better than to do something stupid like this. You're going to have to be punished. I want you to understand that what you did was terribly wrong."

"Jimmy could've died, for God's sake," her mother said. "And you could've been raped, or killed."

"I just wanted to help Jiminy." Elizabeth couldn't hold herself up anymore; her shoulders slumped and tears flooded her eyes.

Her mother considered her for a moment and then handed her a handkerchief. "You've behaved absolutely atrociously, I want you to realize that. I don't want to think what could've happened to him. To both of you. You've got to promise me faithfully that you'll never ever do anything so stupid again. Do you hear me?"

"I promise." Elizabeth blew her nose.

"I say we all head to the kitchen for a nice cup of tea, maybe even a sundowner," her father said. "It has been a long, long day."

That night, Jiminy had his milk and vomited. It took another three days of that before her mother and father decided to try goat's milk. They borrowed Jessie, the nanny goat, from Mr. Osborne. Jessie soon became a permanent resident. But it took a rash under Jiminy's arms and in between his toes that grew into oozing sores for her mother to give the *muti* in the Zambuck tin a try, but by then she was willing to risk him turning brown again. To Elizabeth's relief it didn't change his color, and the rash cleared up.

Elizabeth's punishment had been set at three weeks: no leaving the house under any circumstance, which included the weekly trips she usually took with her dad to the curing sheds.

Of course, her lessons with Mr. Coetzee went on unabated. With nothing else to do but study, she passed her history test with flying colors a week later.

Ten days into her punishment, she got a reprieve of sorts. And it was because of Chipo. He had contracted dysentery the day before and was back in the *kraal* recuperating. Her mother had no one to help her prepare for the belated Federation party they were supposed to have hosted on the day they divvied up the supplies. Wanting to show everyone she was up to the task, her mother had agreed to the party right after Jiminy started sleeping through the night.

It was up to Elizabeth to help her mother prepare for the party. With nothing else to do besides study for her test, she'd thrown herself into cleaning the house. All around her, the furniture, shelves, knickknacks, and walls fairly glowed from all of her scrubbing, dusting, and polishing efforts.

Unfortunately, there had been a couple of accidents. She'd broken two of her mother's most prized possessions: her grandmother's intricately carved ivory lion clutching a monkey in its mouth, and a teacup from the old lady's tea set.

Now, with the midday sun creating geometric patterns across the red concrete floor, Elizabeth was busy scraping built-up floor wax from the baseboard with a kitchen knife. She found herself looking forward to the party. Something different. Across the room, her mother was on hands and knees, dusting beneath the display case. She was dressed in an old, faded housedress and an apron, her hair tied up in a ribbon.

"Bloody Chipo," her mother said, "I didn't think it was possible, but he's worse than bloody Nelson for not cleaning behind and under things."

Nelson. Turu's father. He was still in prison. Elizabeth hadn't thought about him for a while. The only time his name came up was when her mother was angry with Chipo.

Her father stuck his head around the doorway. "I fixed the iron and milked Jessie." He stopped and did a double take at the curls of old wax on the floor next to Elizabeth, then strode into the middle of the room and looked around. He whistled softly. "Whoa, maybe we should fire Chipo and let you—"

"Yoo-hoo," a voice trilled from the kitchen. "Where *is* everybody?"

Mrs. Emily Bradley. Elizabeth glanced at her mother. Hopefully this wouldn't mean an argument between her parents.

Her mother flapped a hand at her father and stumbled to her feet. "Don't let her in here." She undid the ribbon around her hair, retied it, and squinting at her reflection in the window, scrubbed at a smear on her cheek.

Her father headed for the door. But it was too late. Mrs. Bradley's backless shoes echoed through the house.

Her mother glared at her father. "You didn't lock the door?"

"Oh, you're home! What a pleasant surprise." Mrs. Bradley appeared in the doorway and gave her father a blinding smile. She was wearing a light-blue dress, her lips painted bright red. "I hope you don't mind—I showed myself in."

"What brings you here?" her father asked in a bluff, hearty tone.

"I just dropped in to ask a favor. Well, actually, it's—" She stopped and, with a glance around the room, angled her head toward her mother. "Oh, you poor thing. I heard about Chipo. Why didn't you send word? I would've brought Lindani with me to help you."

Her mother's eyes flashed. "Elizabeth and I are managing quite nicely, thank you."

"How about I make us all a nice cup of tea?" Her father asked.

"I'd prefer a tot of brandy." Mrs. Bradley waited a moment, then grinned. "Oh, I'm just playing. You know me."

Jiminy let out a wail.

Mrs. Bradley's blue eyes widened. "Uh oh. I do hope I didn't wake the poor little thing."

"I'll go see to Jimmy." Her father almost sprinted across the room toward the bedroom. "You ladies visit awhile."

Her mother glared at his back before turning to Mrs. Bradley with a pasted-on smile. "So, Emily, may I get you that cup of tea, then?"

"Oh, my heavens, no. I don't want to be any trouble—"

"No trouble at all. I'll just go and put on the kettle." Her mother turned on her heel. "Please, make yourself comfortable. I'll be right back."

Elizabeth jumped to her feet and beat her mother to the door. She wasn't going to stay and entertain Mrs. Bradley, not for anything. She charged into the kitchen, plugged in their new electric kettle, and started pulling out cups. Hurrying in behind her, her mother grabbed a dishtowel and threw it over the dirty dishes in the sink.

Mrs. Bradley followed them in. "The reason I stopped by was to ask Mac a favor. Lloyd's not going to be able to make it back in time from Jo'burg, so he wanted him to do the Gwelo run tomorrow."

"Jo'burg?" Her mother reached for the tea canister.

Elizabeth spread a napkin over their one and only tray and arranged three cups and saucers and teaspoons on it.

"It was a last-minute decision." Mrs. Bradley pulled out a chair, gave it a swipe with one gloved hand, and sat down. "He had a meeting yesterday with some tobacco people."

"Ladyfingers?" Her mother asked.

"Oh no, thank you. I'm watching my waistline."

"I'll take a couple of those." Her father strode into the kitchen, jiggling a squirming and fussing Jiminy.

"There's the little one!" Mrs. Bradley twisted around in her chair to look at Jiminy. Her face melted into an expression of exaggerated concern. "Oh dear, the poor little creature. I thought his allergies had cleared up."

"They have." Her father shot an anxious glance at her mother "We've got this *muti* that's just worked wonders. This is a new outbreak. By tomorrow, it will be gone."

"I'm so glad." Mrs. Bradley leaned forward and grasped Jiminy by the foot. "Such a tiny little bloke, aren't you? My goodness, when my boys were this age they were huge. I could barely hold them—"

"Lemon with your tea?" her mother said.

Mrs. Bradley glanced at her watch and rose to her feet. "Oh my goodness, look at the time. Would it be so terribly rude of me if I didn't stay for tea? I really ought to go. I have to get a package on the train and then run over to Mrs. Coetzee, she's making a dress for me for the party."

"Don't give it another moment's thought," her mother said. "I'm so sorry you can't stay."

Mrs. Bradley turned to her father. "I was just telling Annie, Lloyd won't be back in time from Jo'burg tomorrow to do the Gwelo run. Would you mind?"

"Not at all." Her father swung a now-whining Jiminy in larger and larger arcs.

"Well, then. Until the party." Mrs. Bradley turned to go. She glanced back at her mother with that same look of exaggerated concern she'd shown Jiminy. "Now don't be too proud to ask for help, you hear?"

Her mother's hands clenched, and for a moment Elizabeth thought she might shout at Mrs. Bradley. Instead, she managed to say in a voice that shook only slightly around the edges, "I'm managing quite nicely. Thank you all the same."

"Ta, ta, then," Mrs. Bradley said over her shoulder.

Her mother and father murmured polite good-byes, and then the dreadful woman was gone. The kettle began to boil. Elizabeth pulled out the plug.

Her mother turned to glare at her father. "'Oh, you're home. What a pleasant surprise.' Ha! She knew you'd be home for lunch. Probably hoping I had taken off for the hills."

"Well, she did need to ask me to do the Gwelo—"

"'I'd prefer a nice tot of brandy'?"

"It's not my fault she asked for brandy."

Her mother stalked over to the sideboard and picked up her pack of cigarettes. She withdrew one, lit it, inhaled deeply, and then poked the glowing end at Mac. "Do you know how many times she called me 'you poor thing'? Twice! Oh, and did you hear her call Jimmy a poor *creature*?"

Jiminy's lip quivered and he burst out crying.

"It's okay, little man." Her father patted him on the back. "Mommy's not mad at you."

Her mother stubbed her cigarette out in an ashtray on the table and then took Jiminy into her arms. "Sorry, love. Mommy's so sorry for giving you a fright. So sorry." Her eyes filled with tears.

Her father patted her on the shoulder. "There, there, it's all right."

"No, it's not." Her mother sniffled, pressing Jiminy's head against her cheek. "That stupid bloody woman, I can just hear her telling Mrs. Coetzee what an old hag I look like, and how I can't take care of my baby or my house. They don't even invite me to their tea parties anymore. Maybe it's just as well. I can't stand to see the pity in their eyes when they look at Jiminy." She hugged him tighter.

Her father slid his arm around her shoulder. "Here, let me take him while you go and blow your nose and wash your face."

"I'm all right."

"Come on, now, just let me take him." Easing Jiminy from her arms, he motioned for Elizabeth to hand him the pacifier on the kitchen cabinet. "Come, son, how's about some gripe water?"

Elizabeth knew what to do. In minutes, the pacifier soaked in gripe water was in Jiminy's mouth. Her father rocked Jiminy from side to side until his sobs subsided to sporadic shudders.

Her mother reached into her pocket, withdrew her hankie, and blew her nose. "Oh, my God, I must look a terrible fright."

"No, you really don't," her father said. "You look quite beautiful."

"Honestly!" Her mother rolled her eyes, but Elizabeth could tell she was pleased. Her mother headed for the counter. "I don't know about you, but I'm ready for this cup of tea."

"How about we let Elizabeth take Jiminy back to his crib and sit with him for a while," her father asked. "See if she can get him back to sleep, hey? We can have our tea together, and then I really must get back to work."

"Please, Mom? I know I can get him to sleep." Ever since her escapade, she'd been pressing her mother to let her help more with Jiminy.

"I don't know . . ."

"I can do it," Elizabeth said. "Honestly. I promise."

Her mother nodded with pursed lips. "All right, then. Thanks."

Her father eased a loudly sucking Jiminy into Elizabeth's arms.

"Nice gripe water, hey?" she whispered, cradling him. He rewarded her with a heavy-lidded, satisfied look. She headed toward her parents' bedroom. "Just like old times, hey, Jiminy Timiny?"

"Shall I bring you your tea?" her father asked.

"No thanks, I'll have it later."

Reaching her parents' bedroom, with its perpetually drawn curtains, she stood rocking her brother. She enjoyed having sole custody of him again, even if only for a short while. He made small grunting sounds.

"We can't keep on going like this," her father said from the kitchen. "Doc Goodwin said Jimmy's going to need the kind of care he can't give him."

Elizabeth's ears pricked up. Muffled words. Silence. More garbled words. She kept rocking Jiminy until his eyes closed, then eased him into his crib. He jerked, his eyes fluttered open briefly, he gave a cry and then, wildly sucking on his pacifier, he fell back asleep. She patted his stomach and shushed him. He began to snore. His pacifier slipped from his mouth.

She'd done it! She'd put him to sleep.

Keeping one eye on Jiminy, she tiptoed to the door.

"You know our best bet is to go back to Nkana," her father said.

She stopped. Nkana.

The Northern Rhodesian copper-mining town where she'd been born. She felt a rush of excitement. She was seven when they left for South Africa, and they had lived with her mother's parents for two years before moving here, to the sisal plantation. She crept into the hallway to hear more.

"But we can get him much better medical treatment in South Africa," her mother said.

"Annie, please be reasonable. It costs too much down there. You know we can't afford the kind of care he's going to need."

Silence.

"I could ask my parents to help—"

"Absolutely not. Come on, you don't want that. *I* know you don't. *You* know you don't, and I certainly don't. It won't be that bad, you'll see. Let's face it, the money's good up in Nkana. We'll qualify for a three-bedroom house, and Elizabeth won't have to go away to boarding school. She'll have girls her own age to play with, and we'll be right in town if Jimmy suddenly takes ill. Plus, we'll have the specialists we need, free of charge."

Elizabeth could barely contain her excitement.

No boarding school. No more sour Mr. Coetzee. Instead, a real school with other girls, swimming baths, a cinema, a bookshop. Maybe even her best friend, Deirdre, would still be there.

Then it struck her. She'd never see Turu again. Nor Anesu. And then there was the amulet. And the blue fairies.

Her mother's voice broke into her thoughts.

"She threw herself into helping me. I mean, you saw how much work she did. I was very pleased. But I definitely had to keep an eye on her. You know how rough she is with things. Do you know she broke my grandmother's little ivory lion? Actually it was the little monkey in its mouth, she broke it right off. That was such a masterful piece of carving. So very intricate and donkey's years old. Oh, and not only that, she broke the handle off one of the teacups from my grandmother's tea set. I had to fight to get that tea set, and now it's ruined. Honestly, I was so mad I wanted to strangle her. I think her punishment has been more of a punishment for me."

"Listen, why don't I take her with me to Gwelo tomorrow, to get her out of your hair?"

Elizabeth held her breath. *Please, oh please, Mom.*

"Well . . . I suppose so."

Elizabeth did a little dance in the doorway. Jiminy whimpered in his sleep. She tiptoed back to him, gently rubbed his tummy, and then eased his pacifier back into his mouth. Making little sucking sounds, he sank back into sleep.

Elizabeth began making plans for the following day's trip. Maybe she'd even persuade her father to buy her a Pepsi and an ice-cream sandwich at the café down the street from Economy Stores, where they would be doing most of their shopping.

Chapter 18

A FTER A QUICK BREAKFAST OF TEA AND TOAST WITH butter and jam, Elizabeth and her father left for Gwelo. The sun was just beginning its climb up the water tower at the edge of the Bradleys' yard. Elizabeth wore the amulet, but kept it hidden beneath her dress.

The road to Gwelo lay draped over the undulating hills like a ribbon tossed on an unmade bed. Ten miles along, they stopped to watch a mom and baby sable buck grazing not forty feet from the road. To while away the time, they played games like, I Spy, and ate the ladyfingers her father had sneaked from her mother's hoard. Elizabeth also took a pee break behind a baobab tree, and together they skimmed rocks across the Bondo River at a bridge. The three hours passed quickly.

They arrived in Gwelo on Bulawayo Avenue, the town's main thoroughfare; two tarred lanes separated by a dirt median splashed with clumps of orange cannas. Evenly spaced concrete streetlamps with long metal arms reached over both lanes in an inverted *W* like herons about to land.

Her father parked in the dirt in front of a block-long string of five stores beneath a blooming jacaranda tree. They emerged from the Ford stretching and yawning, and stepped up onto the uneven concrete pavement that ran the length of the stores. Her father led the way into Economy Stores, a one-story brick building.

It was packed with everything from farm implements to brooms and buckets, dishes and glasses, bolts of cloth, knitting wool, and knickknacks. Shelves lined the walls and filled the two aisles, which were separated by wooden counters. The place smelled like Mr. van Zyl's shop—except there was more cigarette smoke, generated by the ten or so white women and men standing at the various counters ordering goods, with a few small children in tow.

Her father headed across the concrete floor toward the back of the shop where the groceries were kept. He shouted greetings to a few of the men along the way. Elizabeth strolled after him, hungry for the sight of every little thing, reaching out to run her hand over a bolt of cloth, and stopping to touch a porcelain figurine of a puppy bowed in play.

She finally reached him again and hugged his side while he ordered the month's supplies, waiting for an opportunity to slip in her request for a jar of pickled onions and a Peppermint Crisp.

Two hours later, after making nearby stops at the butcher, the chemist, and the bottle store for gin and CO_2 cartridges for their seltzer bottle, Elizabeth and her father headed for the corner café for the promised ice-cream sandwich and Pepsi.

Her father stopped at Edgar's Shoe Shop. "Hang on, Bitty. I'm just going to pop in here for a minute, see if I can get them to fix my shoe."

"Da-ad!"

"Come on, come in with me. It won't take long, I promise."

"I'll wait." She wandered around for a moment, then sank down onto a nearby rock for some people-watching.

Across the side road on a dusty sidewalk, a gaunt black man around twenty or so was pacing up and down, dust puffing up with every step he took. Every once in a while, he dropped into a crouch like a warrior hunting a lion, and then the next moment he was upright, cocking his head like he was a big boss or something. A clump of young African men stood watching him, their mouths slightly open.

Elizabeth glanced around for a white landowner or policeman, amazed he was getting away with this kind of behavior. He didn't seem at all worried about the consequences of an African acting out in public. And . . . there was something familiar about the man.

The amulet beneath her blouse suddenly felt warm, alive, like a fist pressed against her breastbone. She slowly rose to her feet and, reaching down into her blouse, lifted it out.

What was happening?

As if in slow motion, the man across the street stopped in midpace and turned toward her, his eyes pinpoints of black light that burned into her.

She gasped and dropped the amulet. She'd seen those eyes before. The apparition in the yard!

The man's gaze followed the amulet, now lying against her dress. He stared at it, transfixed for a moment, then looked up at her, some kind of fury building in him. The air crackled. The group edged away.

"Hey *kaffir*, who the hell do you think you're looking at?"

The man swung around. So did Elizabeth. A white man about the same age as her father strode toward the group, outrage on his face. The group scattered. Without waiting to see what happened, Elizabeth ran toward Edgar's Shoe Shop.

"How dare you look at the *picannin dona* like that!" the man shouted behind her.

She charged into the store, blinking sun-blinded eyes around for her father. He stood on the far left of the store, examining a black shoe. She ran to him and threw her arms around his waist.

"Bitty!" He replaced the shoe and wrapped his arms around her. "What—"

"Oh, Daddy! I was so scared."

He craned his neck to look outside. "What happened?"

"I saw the man that . . ." But what was she going to tell him? That she'd seen the man who had magicked his way into their storage shed?

"What man?" He lifted her chin. "Where? What did he do?"

"It-it was just this *munt* who was shouting and . . . and acting crazy, and it frightened me."

"Come on." He grabbed her hand and started toward the door. "Point him out to me."

She pulled him back. "Uh, no. He's probably gone by now. It's all right. He didn't do anything to me, I was just frightened." She didn't want to risk seeing the man again. Just the sight of him made her feel weak and more afraid than she'd ever felt in her life. Besides, what could her father possibly do? From what she'd seen before she ran, the white man had probably sorted the man out.

"Are you sure?"

"Honest."

"We-ll, as long as he didn't do anything to you." He pulled her toward the door. "Let's go and have ourselves a Pepsi and an ice-cream sandwich."

At the door to the shoe shop, Elizabeth risked a peek toward where the man had been holding court. There was no one around. It was as if the incident had never happened. She took a step outside. Rain clouds blossomed out of nowhere. A flash of lightening split the sky, and in moments the ground thrummed with rain pelting down.

Elizabeth and her father ran into the café and had their treats. Half an hour later, they headed home beneath a dark canopy of clouds and sporadic rain.

Chapter 19

TURURU EYED THE DARKENING SKY FROM INSIDE ANESU'S hut. How long before it poured? He still had to make a trip to the *kraal* to check on his mother. But Anesu told him to wait. She said it was a good time for him to practice reading the bones, what with the energy of the full moon of Chibumbi upon them.

But he knew that wasn't the reason she wanted him to wait. She was afraid to throw the bones alone.

This troubled him. All of her deterioration troubled him. She seemed to be shrinking inside her clothes, and she no longer allowed him to change her bandage. Instead, she changed it when he wasn't around. It must be bad.

At all times of the day and night she'd stop, hold up her wounded hand, and mutter incantations. That worried him most of all. Her eyes were the only part of her that remained the same; they still glowed with that fire that was his true grandmother, but there was great pain there too.

Tururu turned back to face into the hut and headed for the mat where his grandmother sat with her eyes closed, getting ready to throw the bones. Watching her uneasily, he settled down opposite her. Why was she moving her head around like that, like she couldn't get comfortable? And why so many incantations? She had never begun this way before.

Protect me, Amai Vedu," Anesu finally whispered. She opened her eyes and flung the bones across the mat.

They clicked and tumbled against one another and then rolled to a stop. A flash of lightning lit them momentarily. The air vibrated with electricity. Rain pelted down, some of it splashing into the hut. Tururu stared down at the old, yellowed animal bones, noting this one and that and the way they fell. Grandmother had taught him what it all meant, but he'd never been able to "see" into the bones like she did, like a good *godobori* should.

But that day, he felt something stirring inside him. He closed his eyes.

The hazy figure of a man appeared across the window of his mind, pant legs flapping. The man was pacing and up and down. There was something familiar about the figure. A group of men nearby stood watching him.

Anesu cried out. He gave a start and opened his eyes.

Her spirit eye was glowing, like it used to. She was in a trance, staring at a scene he couldn't see. He quickly closed his eyes again, willing the images back.

"He was looking straight at me," Grandmother whispered. "He could see me."

Tururu leaned forward. "Karari?"

"This time, I could feel him. His hatred, it was very strong. I almost didn't recognize him. He has become very thin, and he is growing weaker. It is the *ngozi*. The leaders, they sent him away because they sense his madness. They fear him."

"Where is he?"

"Nearby. Gwelo, maybe," she said absently, then stiffened. "*That* is why the seeing was different. It was through the amulet. The missus was wearing the amulet!"

"Aiyee! He will take it from her."

"Missus is in great danger. You must bring her and the amulet here, to me." She held out her good arm. "Help me up."

Tururu helped her to her feet and over to the table.

"I thought it would be the *ngozi* that would destroy him. But now I see that I must be the one. I don't know how I will do it, but I will do it." She sighed. "I will also have to face the *ngozi*."

She nodded to herself. And then, laying her bad hand on the table, she reached for her knife and raised it.

She was going to cut off her hand!

Tururu lunged for the knife, but she pushed him away with a frown.

"I am cutting off my bandage. I should've done so a long time ago. My wound is never going to heal. I was fooling myself." She slipped the knife between her wrist and the bandage and started to slice.

Tururu held his breath. He hadn't seen her hand since that first week. Sometimes he wondered if there were actual *ngozi* inside there, what with the way the bandage glowed blue all the time.

"I refused to accept that the *ngozi* had become a part of me," Anesu said, as if she had read his mind. "This is the price I paid for losing my temper. I can be like Karari, but I choose not to."

She clipped the last bit of cloth. The bandage fell away.

Tururu gasped. Her hand looked like a blackened chicken claw, the flesh stretched over fused bones. And then, as they both watched, the blue smolder dimmed slightly. Anesu's mouth trembled and she looked up toward Amai Vedu with a grateful smile. She turned to Tururu.

"Listen carefully. Go to missus and do whatever you need to do to bring her and *nadira* back here, or she will surely die. And Karari, along with the *ngozi*, will bring about great destruction to our people."

"But Grandmother, what did you mean about you . . . the *ngozi* . . . ?"

"Not now. There is no time. Go!"

Tururu glanced outside. "It is still raining."

She straightened and glared at him. With a sigh, he collected the old rain hat Elizabeth had given him and set out across a darkened veld. He had a feeling this was not going to be easy.

Chapter 20

DINNER WAS ALREADY OVER BY THE TIME ELIZABETH and her father returned home from Gwelo. The journey back had been a nightmare. It rained most of the way and they got stuck for over an hour after her father tried to gun the Ford through a washed-out section of the road. It was deeper than he realized, and the engine died. With rain pelting down, he removed a little black cap type of thing from the engine, dried it on his shirt, and replaced it. But the Ford still wouldn't start. Half an hour and five attempts later, the car finally coughed to life and they continued down the road at a snail's pace.

When her mother heard about Elizabeth's experience in Gwelo, she insisted that she sleep on a pallet beside their bed.

The following morning, yawning and glancing around uneasily, Elizabeth headed for the chicken coop to gather eggs for the chocolate cake her mother intended to bake for the party. Her mother had been at it since dawn. Chipo still hadn't shown up.

"Psst!"

Heart pounding, Elizabeth dropped behind the corrugated iron side of the coop. She peered around the doorway but couldn't see anything. And then she saw him. Turu, twenty yards away, the top of his head barely visible behind the morning glory fence. She felt nervous and glad and angry all at once. With a glance toward the house, she hunched over and ran behind the fence. Turu sat waiting for her on one knee, like a runner about to take off.

She squatted down in front of him. "What're you doing here?"

He glanced over his shoulder. "Grandmother say missi *must* bring *nadira* back."

"But—"

"Grandmother says missi *must* come with Tururu! There is much danger—"

"Elizabeth!"

Elizabeth scrambled up. "Listen, I have to go. Meet me in the tree house later, okay?"

"No, missi must come *now*."

"I can't just go now, and besides—"

"Eliza-beth! I swear, if I have to come and get you . . ."

She turned to go. He grabbed her hand.

She wrenched away. "The tree house. Later." And then in a louder voice she called, "Coming!"

She had almost reached the back steps before she remembered the eggs. She ran back and collected four.

"Took you long enough," her mother said as she ran huffing into the kitchen.

"Sorry." Elizabeth swatted at the smoke from the cigarette parked on the edge of the counter next to where her mother was creaming butter and sugar.

"Put them in that bowl on the sink. And then would you please go and give Jimmy his pacifier, there's a good girl? Oh, and then hurry back. I want you to sift four cups of flour into that bowl over there for me." Her mother nodded toward the table.

After doing as she was told, Elizabeth headed toward her parents' bedroom, glad to get away from her mother's frenzy.

What was that all about with Turu? Why did Anesu want the amulet back all of a sudden? What had happened? Well, she wasn't ready to return it. Not yet.

She turned into her bedroom and retrieved the amulet from the cigar box she'd slipped it back into after her encounter with Karari in Gwelo. She slid it over her head and went to her parents' bedroom.

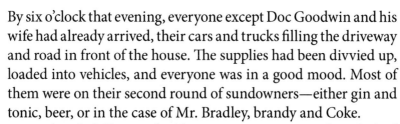

By six o'clock that evening, everyone except Doc Goodwin and his wife had already arrived, their cars and trucks filling the driveway and road in front of the house. The supplies had been divvied up, loaded into vehicles, and everyone was in a good mood. Most of them were on their second round of sundowners—either gin and tonic, beer, or in the case of Mr. Bradley, brandy and Coke.

A ghostly full moon had begun its journey up a sky splashed with fuchsia, gold, and orange above the remains of the sun clinging to the horizon.

Elizabeth wore the blue dress her mother had made for her before Jiminy was born, as well as the multicolored sandals she was allowed to wear on special occasions. Her mother had braided her hair into a tighter-than-usual single plait. The way it pulled the skin back from her face made her feel extra watchful. She'd stayed in her bedroom as long as she could in order to put off facing the Bradley boys, but her mother had finally dragged her out to help carry dishes of food to the table that had been set up on the grass in front of the storeroom.

Mrs. Coetzee and Mrs. Campbell sat chatting on kitchen chairs, feet tucked beneath, glasses of gin and tonic clutched in their laps. Her father, along with Mr. Bradley, Commissioner Campbell, and Mr. Coetzee, stood in a circle around the *braaivleis* drum, drinks in hand. Smoke billowed up from the recently lit coals.

Mr. Bradley was boasting how he had what it took to make a success of growing tobacco. With her father's help, of course. Her father hung back. He must not have told Mr. Bradley about their plans to return to Nkana. Maybe he'd changed his mind. Elizabeth hadn't heard anything more about the subject since that time she'd overheard her parents' conversation.

She glanced around. Where were those Bradley boys? She'd heard their voices but had yet to see them. They'd better not find Turu's wire cars.

She headed for the side of the garage to check, then stopped. A short distance away, in the fading light, the brothers and seven-year-old Danie Coetzee were slinging rocks at a row of empty beer bottles. She did an about-face, headed back around the other way, and peeked in at Turu's cars. Safe enough for now.

Turu. She'd asked him to wait for her in the tree house. That was hours ago. Was he still up there, right now? Surely he wouldn't have risked it.

The screen door squealed and Mrs. Bradley, backless shoes clacking, flounced down the steps and headed for the "bar," an icebox her father had set up against the garage wall. Mr. van Zyl was there, pouring himself a whiskey. He waved the bottle in her direction.

"Yes, please," she called.

Elizabeth headed for the tree house.

"Hey, *kaffir*," Mr. Bradley called.

Elizabeth froze, heart in her throat. She glanced around.

Chipo, hands clasped in front of him, emerged from the shadows near the back of the yard. "Bwana?"

"You don't look so good," her father said.

"So, where the hell have you been then?" Mr. Bradley said, his face jovial from the brandy. "Not a good reflection on your former bwana when you don't show up for work, is it now, hey?"

Chipo lifted one shoulder apologetically. "Chipo sick, bwana."

"Sick my arse." Bradley made a comment to Mr. Coetzee that Elizabeth couldn't hear, and they both laughed.

"He had dysentery, for God's sake," her father said.

"Chipo!" Her mother appeared in the kitchen doorway. "Are you well enough to work?"

"Yes, medem." Chipo hurried toward her.

"Good. Go put on your jacket and then bring out the plates and napkins. They're on the kitchen table." She stopped and eyed him. "You *do* have a clean jacket, don't you?"

"Yes, medem."

"All right then, off you go."

He hurried into Nelson's *kiya*.

Elizabeth slid onto the swing, pushed off, and, pumping her legs, peered up at the shadowy form of the tree house above for signs of Turu. She couldn't see anything. Trying to decide what to do, she continued to swing. Her gaze fell on Mrs. Bradley and Mr. van Zyl still over at the "bar," drinks in hand. Elizabeth hoped Mrs. Bradley would stay occupied and keep away from her father.

Mr. van Zyl leaned over and whispered something in Mrs. Bradley's ear, pinching her bottom at the same time. With a look of fake outrage, she slapped his hand. He raised his glass in a toast. She laughed and clinked her glass against his, then turned and headed for the *braaivleis* pit. Mr. van Zyl watched her leave for a moment, then drew himself up, adjusted the gun in his waistband, and followed her.

"How's the meat coming?" he said to the gathered men.

Mr. Bradley shook his head. "Do you smell any meat cooking, hey?"

Mr. van Zyl wasn't very popular; he wasn't part of the supply-sharing group, what with his own shop. They invited him mostly out of politeness. He always walked over from his place and then staggered home afterward, or just slept in the veld if he passed out before he made it.

Mr. van Zyl peered down at the grill. "Those coals look ready. I'm hungry."

"Have a sausage roll," her father said.

"I wonder where Doc is," Commisioner Campbell said. "It's not like him to be late."

As if conjured up by their conversation, Doc's truck came tearing down the road, its headlights glowing red from the dust. It skidded to a halt in front of the house. Doc bolted from the car and ran toward them, leaving the door hanging open. His wife stared, wild-eyed, from the passenger's seat.

"It's started!" he cried.

Mr. Bradley dropped the stick he was poking the fire with. "What's—"

"The veld. They've set the veld on fire."

"Who has?" her father asked.

"The bloody *kaffirs*, who do you think? There are fires everywhere."

There was a stunned silence for a moment. The veld burned quick as kindling, fire consuming everything in its path. There was no fire department to put it out, no central water system. No way to stop it.

Elizabeth ran to her father and pressed herself against his side. He hugged her close.

"I should've paid more attention when I saw those groups of *kaffirs*." Doc's words tumbled over one another. "Anyway, I'm headed back to my place. Just came by to warn you." He turned and charged back toward his truck.

"I've got to get home," Mrs. Campbell cried, her voice rising with barely suppressed hysteria. "Edward and Mrs. Simpson—"

Elizabeth recognized the names of her two corgis.

"Damn!" Mr. Bradley pointed toward the curing sheds. A thin plume of smoke rose near the buildings that were filled with drying sisal. "If those propane tanks explode, we're done for—and sooner than later."

"Lloyd!" Mrs. Bradley cried. "Is that our place?"

Everyone turned to see smoke curling up from the direction of the Bradley house.

"I've got to get over there." Mr. Bradley started toward his truck. "Mac, get over to the sheds, see what you can do."

"Fire!" the Bradley boys shouted, charging after their father.

"We're going to head home." Mr. Coetzee motioned for his wife and son to follow him. They lived near the river on a rocky incline—probably safe from fire, but you never knew.

Her mother ran to her father. "Please be careful, all right?"

He kissed her on the forehead and, disentangling himself from Elizabeth's grip, kissed her as well. "Of course. Don't worry. I'll be back in a jiffy."

Jiminy let out a shrill cry from the house. Her mother turned and ran to him.

With his wife running ahead of him toward their truck, Commissioner Campbell called from across the yard, "I'll ring BSAP headquarters from the house."

"Mac, I'm coming with you," Mr. van Zyl said.

"You need to stay here to protect the women." Her father hurried toward the Ford. He stopped. "Oh, and keep an eye on Chipo. I don't trust him."

"Where is he?"

Her father swung into the Ford. "Find him. And keep that gun handy." He reversed down the driveway. Mr. van Zyl headed for the *kiya*.

Heart pounding, Elizabeth watched her father disappear. She glanced around. She was all alone in the yard. The smell of smoke was stronger now. How long before the fires reached their house? And what of the rebels?

Turu.

She ran toward the tree. Something rustled nearby. A razor-sharp wire of fear uncoiled in her gut and she stopped.

Turu dropped from the avocado tree. "Run, missi!"

A white-jacketed figure flashed from behind the tree and locked him in a chokehold.

Elizabeth turned to run, but before she could move she was grabbed from behind and spun around to face a pair of sunken eyes. Her stomach lurched at the stench of tobacco and *kaffir* beer.

Karari!

He grabbed her by the throat. "I have come for *nadira*."

"Elizabeth!" Her mother's terrified voice seemed miles away. "Where are you?"

Elizabeth tried to call out, but she couldn't. She could barely breathe.

"I-I don't have it," she croaked.

Karari thrust her back and jammed a finger at the shape of the amulet beneath her dress. "Karari not stupid *muntu.*"

A beam of light from the house played through the darkness. Karari ducked, yanking Elizabeth down in front of him. He locked his forearm around her neck. The light bounced and came to rest on them anyway. Pinned back against him, she squinted into the light.

"Hey, *kaffir*, let the girl go. I'm warning you." Mr. van Zyl stood near the *braaivleis* drum, pistol raised. Her mother and Mrs. Bradley huddled a few feet behind him.

"Mommy!" Elizabeth cried.

The light shifted for a moment, and a shot rang out. There was a cry to her left, and a thud as something hit the ground. She twisted around to see what had happened. Chipo lay spread-eagled on his back, Turu's crumpled form on top of him. Blood covered his temple.

She whimpered.

"Two down," Mr. van Zyl called. "One more to go. The next one will be through your head, *kaffir*. As you can see, I'm an excellent shot."

With a growl, Karari aimed his forefinger in Mr. van Zyl's direction and muttered something.

Mr. van Zyl shot up into the air, then crashed down onto the edge of the table, bounced off, and sprawled facedown on the ground. Crying out, Mrs. Bradley ran to his side.

Elizabeth's mother charged toward them. "Let her go!"

Without warning, Elizabeth elbowed Karari in the ribs. He grunted in surprise but held on. Her mother ran at Karari, trying to claw his face. His fist shot out and she crumpled to the ground.

"Mommy!" Elizabeth struggled to reach her mother. Karari yanked her up by her braid.

A thin, keening sound split the air. The tops of the eucalyptus trees swayed back and forth as if stirred by the breath of a giant. Dust devils around them grew and scattered.

Anesu materialized in a blur and a whoosh.

Chapter 21

S HE GRAZED THE *BRAAIVLEIS* DRUM AS SHE LANDED. IT clattered to the ground, spewing ash and glowing coals. She swung around almost drunkenly, trying to get her bearings, then stopped, her gaze sharp and alert. Blood dripped from a gash in her crippled hand, but she didn't seem to notice.

Karari stepped back in surprise, losing his grip on Elizabeth. She wrenched free and scrambled toward the old woman. He caught her by the ankle before she got too far, yanked her back, and looped his arm around her neck.

"Let the girl go." Anesu planted her feet. "Turn back from back this path, Karari. The amulet will do you no good. It is killing you."

He laughed. "You lie. I have never been more powerful."

"The *ngozi* are—"

"Enough, old woman!" He glanced toward the road. "I have no time for you. My men need me."

"I will try to help you if you let me."

"You can help Karari, old woman? Look at yourself. Karari doesn't need anybody's help. Karari will lead our people to greatness."

"You cannot take *nadira*. You know what will happen."

He snorted. "That was before."

"I tell you, Karari, Amai Vedu will not allow it. You *will* die."

Karari hesitated, but then he grabbed Elizabeth's braid and twisted her head, forcing her to look at her mother lying limp on the ground. "No matter. This one will give Karari *nadira* if she wants that one to live."

Elizabeth whimpered. "Mommy . . ."

Karari yanked her head back and turned her face to his. She closed her eyes, faint with terror and pain.

"Please, missus," Anesu said in a low, urgent voice. "You must *not* give Karari *nadira*."

Karari tightened his grip. "Look at me. You *will* give it to me now!"

The edges of Elizabeth's vision darkened. She was going to vomit. She just wanted all of this to stop.

Next to her, Karari seemed to vibrate in place. "Now!"

Hands shaking, Elizabeth reached up for the hide band holding the amulet.

"No, missi!" Turu stumbled from the shadows, his face covered in blood. "Do not give Karari *nadira*. He will still kill medem. He will kill us all."

Elizabeth hesitated.

Karari snapped her head back. "*Nadira*."

Razor-sharp lines of pain seared through Elizabeth's already-throbbing temples. Rockets burst across her vision, and something inside her exploded. Jerking back, she spat in Karari's face.

He jammed the heel of his palm against her cheek with one hand and grabbed the amulet with the other.

Yanked forward, she held on to the band with both hands. "No! You can't have it!"

The milky-white eye of the amulet flashed, and the air shimmered. A stream of golden light poured from the amulet through Karari's fingers and rose in the air. Changing shape as it flowed upward, the light grew until it coalesced into a fiery, birdlike creature. Great talons extended, its feathers glowed red and yellow and gold.

The magnificent creature hung above them for a moment, then flapped its enormous wings, stirring up dust. The bird gave a piercing scream that echoed across the veld, followed by answering calls from hyenas, jackals, and dogs. It plunged toward Karari.

He screamed. The sickening smell of burned flesh filled the air. The fiery bird flowed back into the glowing soapstone amulet gripped in Karari's hand. He flung it from him and gaped down in horror at the image of the amulet that had been seared into his palm, the edges smoking.

Elizabeth stumbled back. The amulet fell harmlessly back against her chest.

"*Ngozi*," Turu whispered, eyes wide.

Elizabeth tore her gaze away from Karari and looked down at the coals that had been flung across the ground when Anesu materialized. Blue and orange flamelike figures danced across the spilled coals lying between them and Karari.

Karari had seen them too. Face contorted with pain, he steadied himself, clutched his injured hand against his chest, and lifted the other in their direction. With his voice breaking, he muttered an incantation. Chittering like a flock of birds, the fire spirits rose in a column in front of him and hung there in a glorious, fiery display. He stared at them through a mask of agony and fascination.

Anesu pulled Elizabeth and Turu to her side. "Help me. I cannot do this alone."

Taking a deep breath, she lifted her clawlike hand. And then, using her other hand as support, she held it out to Karari in a conciliatory gesture. Blue sparks flashed through the streaks of blood covering her claw. Shaking with the effort, she kept her hand extended, all the while muttering an incantation. Sweat beaded her forehead.

"Karari, please," she said in a broken voice. "It does not have to end this way."

Whispering and hissing, the *ngozi* swayed back and forth between Anesu's claw and Karari's extended hand.

Tearing his eyes off the *ngozi*, Karari screamed another incantation and stabbed his hand in Anesu's direction. The fire spirits streamed up and, in a hissing wave, surged toward Anesu.

She lifted her blue, pulsing, misshapen hand with great effort even higher and closed her eyes. She seemed resigned. Elizabeth huddled against her, mesmerized as the blue, fairylike creatures poured toward them.

And then, as if hitting an invisible wall, the *ngozi* stopped, hung in the air for a moment, then turned and made a beeline back toward Karari. He froze, his eyes almost popping out of his head, and turned to run.

But before he could move, the *ngozi* swarmed all over him.

In a magnificent display of orange and blue, and with a greedy murmuring and whispering that sounded nearly human, the fire spirits wrapped him in an almost loving-looking embrace. Their chattering became a quiet roar. The bursts of blue and orange fire grew with each of his screams.

Moments later, all that remained of him was a smoldering pile of ash with a few blue, flamelike figures dancing over it.

A sudden distant explosion shook the earth, breaking the spell.

Elizabeth swung around. Smoke billowed up from the curing sheds. "Daddy!"

Anesu grabbed her hand. "Come, missus, you must help. We have no time to waste." She held out her claw to Turu. "Do you remember the incantation for rain?"

He gave a hesitant nod and clasped his grandmother's damaged hand.

Elizabeth felt an electric charge as the three of them linked together. Anesu lifted her face to the sky and began to chant, her voice weak and cracked. Turu haltingly joined in. A light surrounded them as a clap of thunder sounded, close. Their voices rose. A second clap of thunder rumbled in the distance.

They repeated the incantation, louder this time. Another clap of thunder came, even closer this time. Elizabeth joined in even though she didn't know the words.

Bring the rain, she begged.

Raising their hands, they kept chanting. A thick, dark cloud formed above them, obscuring the stars. The smoke-enshrouded moon cast an eerie, reddish light.

A few large drops fell on their outstretched hands.

Anesu took a deep breath and began another invocation; this time her voice was a little stronger. Banks of dark clouds grew until they blotted out the moon. Lightning burst across the sky, followed by rolling thunder.

By the third invocation, Anesu's voice rang out as if all the ancestors were there, helping her.

The sky split open and rain streamed down. Anesu released their hands and flung out her arms as if to embrace the sky. She laughed. Elizabeth did the same, opening her mouth to catch the drops. The rain continued to pour down as if it never intended to stop. Elizabeth splashed through the mud puddles that were rapidly forming. Turu joined in. Elizabeth turned toward Anesu, and gasped. It seemed as if each drop that fell on her blackened, shriveled hand was turning it smooth and supple again.

Anesu gazed down at her hand, and then, hesitantly at first, she began to wiggle her fingers. She spread them wide in a triumphant fan and lifted both hands to the sky. Arms still raised, tears began running down her face. They mingled with the rain as she began a slow tribal dance, her bare feet slapping up and down in the mud. Elizabeth stared at her in astonishment. She had never seen any African woman do that dance before, let alone one so old and weak.

As suddenly as the downpour started, it stopped. The violent storm became a gentle blessing, with only the echoes of the energy that had surged through and around them remaining, along with the sound of rainwater dripping off leaves.

In the sudden break after everything that had happened, Elizabeth remembered her mother and swung around.

"Mommy!"

There was no answer. Elizabeth squinted into the darkness. Her mother still lay on the ground where she'd landed after Karari punched her. She wasn't moving. Elizabeth dropped down beside her.

"Annie? Elizabeth?" Mrs. Bradley called from the house. "Are you all right?"

Elizabeth couldn't answer.

Anesu sank down beside Elizabeth and pressed her ear against her mother's chest.

"Is she dead?" Elizabeth whispered.

Anesu shook her head.

"But she's not moving. Will she be all right?"

Anesu didn't answer; instead, she closed her eyes and held her hands a few inches above her mother's chest, as if warming them over a fire. Then, lifting her chin, she murmured something. She sat silently for what seemed like ages before finally opening her eyes.

"Medem will be all right."

"Annie?" Mrs. Bradley's tremulous voice rang out, this time a little closer.

"Missus, we must go." Anesu grasped Turu's hand. She muttered a few words and, in a shimmer, they disappeared.

Elizabeth stared at where they'd stood.

"Elizabeth?" her mother whispered.

Elizabeth swung around. "Mom! Oh, I'm so glad you're all right!"

Chapter 22

THREE DAYS LATER, ELIZABETH SAT SLUMPED AGAINST one of the plywood walls of her tree house, staring into space. The whole world still smelled of ashes and charred wood. A trapped fly buzzed noisily in a corner. She'd just washed the dishes, swept the floors, and made her bed.

With Chipo dead and no servant to replace him, she was doing more to help her mom around the house. The rooster gave a hesitant cock-a-doodle-doo, but it was already midmorning. Poor thing. Like everyone else, it had been off-kilter ever since the fire. She thought back to everything that had happened since then.

The best thing had been seeing her dad come rushing into the house half an hour after the explosion. He'd done his best to extinguish the blaze, but the fire had grown too big by the time he got to the sheds. When he saw flames snaking out of the structure that housed the propane tanks, he got out of there. Mr. Bradley lost his whole operation but still had most of the sisal plants themselves. He was already busy planning to plant tobacco, with an offer to her dad to return if the mine job didn't pan out.

According to the BSAP, a number of fires had been set around the valley. The captain's assessment was that they had not been very well planned: "Stupid bloody *kaffirs*, probably drunk. Didn't they realize their own village could've gone up as well?"

Everyone agreed that the miraculous downpour had saved them, appearing as it did out of nowhere. They'd have all been done for without it. The BSAP had already made a couple of arrests, but mainly of known troublemakers. Everyone had been surprised by Chipo's involvement. "Such an obedient boy," they said. "Goes to show you, you never know with these buggers."

Except for *The Gwelo Herald*, the fire hadn't made any of the newspapers, but they had covered Joshua Nkomo's arrest in Bulawayo when he tried unsuccessfully to get an audience with the prime minister. When he was informed he wouldn't, he refused to leave.

The toolshed behind Bradleys' house had burned to the ground, as well as their guesthouse. The Campbell's government-subsidized place had sustained enough damage that they'd been moved to temporary quarters in Gwelo. Fortunately, they'd been in time to rescue their corgis, Edward and Mrs. Simpson. Doc Goodwin's clinic and attached house, which was farther down the road on the way to Gwelo, escaped any damage, as the fire hadn't spread that far before the rain. But there were parts of the veld between the Bradleys' house and theirs that looked as if some giant had gone mad with a blowtorch, turning acacia trees into charred sticks. Other areas, including the Shona ruins and the McKenzie house, had been spared.

Van Zyl's shop had escaped the fires as well, with its brick walls and corrugated-metal roof. So had the big baobab. Though it had been singed, because of its watery insides and smooth bark it didn't go up in flames like the other trees. It might even have helped save his place, they said. Otherwise, he would've been homeless as well as laid up.

Poor Mr. van Zyl. He'd been terribly banged up—three cracked ribs, a dislocated jaw, and a broken arm. Elizabeth liked him a little better for trying to rescue her. But she really couldn't get over how her mother had risked her own life to save her. She still sported a huge bruise on her jaw, along with a hazy memory of the night's events. Doc said it was because she'd suffered a mild concussion. As for Mrs. Bradley, her version of the night's events was met with skepticism, the ravings of a drunk and hysterical woman. This made it easier for Elizabeth—there wasn't any way she could've explained what happened. Anytime anyone questioned her, she let herself get teary-eyed and vague, and they'd pat her hand and tell her not to try and remember, that it was all in the past.

But she remembered everything the amulet had done, clear as day.

Elizabeth felt it beneath her dress and wondered once again why Anesu hadn't taken it back. Perhaps she'd meant for Elizabeth to keep it forever. She hoped so, especially since they were to return to Nkana in just six weeks. She wanted something to remember Anesu and Turu by.

What she really wanted, though, was for her family to stay there on the veld, even with the prospect of boarding school looming. She wanted to be able to return to Anesu and Turu on school holidays. That would make it all worth it.

As if conjured up by the amulet, Turu's head appeared through the open trapdoor of the tree house. She jumped. "You gave me a fright!"

He grinned and pulled himself up into the tree house, then crawled over to the space that served as a window and peeked out. "It's all right. My dad's with Mr. Bradley, and my mom's washing clothes in the bathroom."

He nodded and settled against the wall opposite her. She felt a shyness between them, as if what they'd gone through had been too personal.

She leaned over and squinted at his temple. "I can barely even see a mark there."

"Grandmother's *muti*."

"And your grandmother's hut—is it all right, then? Did it burn?"

"No, missi." He flashed her that look that made her feel stupid for asking, like she should've known that nothing could harm a magic hut.

"We're leaving for Nkana, you know," she said. "Soon."

He nodded. "Grandmother see in the bones."

"What else did she see?"

"Elizabeth!" Her mother called.

Turu froze.

"Wait here," she whispered. "I'll quickly go and see what she wants."

"Turu must go." He kept his eyes on the trapdoor. "Missi must come to Anesu, tomorrow."

"Elizabeth, I know you're up there."

"Coming!" She slid toward the trapdoor and dangled her legs over the edge. "But what if I can't, um, you know . . . find the hut again?"

"Grandmother say that missi *will* find hut."

"But, what if I get lost and I—"

"There you are," her mother said from beneath the tree. "I need you to come and help me hang the washing."

"Be down in a jiff!" Giving Turu one last anxious look, she started down the tree.

Chapter 23

IT WAS TWO DAYS BEFORE ELIZABETH WAS ABLE TO SNEAK
out. Her chance came the afternoon of Jiminy's appointment
with Doc Goodwin. Ordinarily she would've been dragged
along, but seeing as how Doc was just down the road visiting a
native clinic, they let her stay home with a promise to lock all the
doors and stay put until they got back.

She set out as soon as the Ford disappeared down the road.

Under a hazy sun and accompanied by the screech of crickets,
she hurried down the path leading through the sisal and to the
open veld, glancing over her shoulder as she went. She hadn't
been out of the yard since the incident with Karari. Patches of
dark gray, rain-tamped ash lay here and there between the rows
of sisal and on the swordlike leaves. She prayed she wouldn't
come across any charred animal carcasses.

Mr. van Zyl's place came in to view, its corrugated roof a dull
silver speck against the blackened horizon. She reminded herself
to take him a nice present before they left for Nkana.

Just past the ruins, she stopped and scanned the fire-scarred veld. Nothing looked familiar. Tamping down a feeling of panic, she reached for the amulet, taking comfort from it.

She plunged ahead, across the thorn-filled scrub. There was that bush from before. It had survived the fire. Thank goodness it was still there. And there was the first knoll. She strode up the incline. Before long she could see the charred remains of the black monkey thorn tree at the top of the next rise.

Almost there.

Holding her thumbs for extra luck, she charged up the hill and looked down the other side, almost expecting to see the hut nestled where she'd left it. But there was nothing but miles of blackened veld.

Trying to ignore the wave of anxiety that rose in her chest, she took a deep breath, closed her eyes, and with all her might reached out with her heart and her mind to Anesu.

"Come forth, oh great hut!"

Flies buzzed around her head. She swatted them away and opened her eyes.

There stood Anesu's hut, just as she'd left it.

She gave a whoop. There was the same old well and thorn tree, the same old nanny goat, this time curled up on the ground near the fire pit, where a big, black pot—

She stopped. The fire.

There was the very same blue-tinged fire filled with the same little demons that had almost killed them, the demons that had devoured Karari. She shuddered. How could the old woman still keep something like that right in her front yard? She charged down the hill, giving the fire a wide berth.

Turu appeared in the hut's doorway. "Missi!"

"I found it! Just like you said."

He grinned. "Grandmother waiting."

Elizabeth followed him into the hut. Her eyes quickly adjusted to the change from bright sunlight. Ahh.

The interior glowed with its own magic light. Everything else was as she remembered as well: the same smooth mud walls, the same dirt floor, the same old jam, pickle, and mayonnaise jars filled with their mysterious concoctions lined up on the same old table where Anesu had mixed the *muti* for Jiminy's rash. And no flies. She glanced back toward the doorway at the flies buzzing around outside. She breathed deeply. The same old smell of wood and smoke. And something else. Bacon?

"*Picannin dona*," Anesu said.

Elizabeth turned to see the old woman sitting on a mat near her mattress. It was a very different Anesu who greeted her. The face gazing up at her from beneath a new striped *douk* wasn't gray and drawn any more. There was a shine to her dark skin, and energy seemed to hum around her.

"Hello," Elizabeth said, suddenly shy.

"Come, missus." Anesu motioned Elizabeth to sit opposite her.

Elizabeth hesitated. What else was different about Anesu from the last time she'd been here? Of course. Her hand. Elizabeth flashed back to that moment when the rain had poured down, healing Anesu's scarred hand. It hadn't been a dream, after all.

"Come-come, missus, sit." Anesu smiled and patted the mat.

Elizabeth plopped down and crossed her legs. The doorway darkened and Turu hurried in carrying two large, steaming enameled bowls. He kneeled and set them down in the middle of the mat, then sat down between Elizabeth and Anesu.

Elizabeth recognized what was in one bowl. *Sadza*. She grinned. She loved the stiff cooked cornmeal—no one made it better than the Africans did. She glanced curiously at the mound of crispy little curls in the other bowl. That must have been what she'd smelled before. Except this didn't look like bacon. Fried lizards? Was that a little eye peering up at her?

Suppressing a shudder, she started to ask what it was, then remembered her manners.

Anesu murmured something in Shona. Turu jumped up and ran outside again, this time returning with a small bowl of warm grease. Placing it beside the *sadza*, he sat back down, grabbed a handful of the crispies, and popped them into his mouth. Anesu helped herself to them as well. They crunched noisily, mouths open.

"Missus?" Anesu nodded toward the bowl.

"Oh, not right now, thank you." She thought if she waited long enough maybe they'd finish the strange little morsels.

She reached over and scooped a small handful of *sadza*, molded it into a ball, pressed her thumb in the middle, dipped it in the grease, and popped it into her mouth. Just like old times. She hadn't eaten *sadza* like this since those evenings back in Nkana with their servant Leffy, when they'd squatted around his cooking fire behind their house on Tenth Avenue.

That reminded her. She wiped the grease from her mouth with the back of her hand. "Turu told me you saw in the bones that we're going back to Nkana."

Anesu nodded.

"I'm not at all pleased about it, mind you." Elizabeth reached for more *sadza*.

Anesu thrust the bowl of curlies toward her. "Come-come, missus, eat! It is very good."

Elizabeth gulped. She couldn't refuse now. It would be rude. Anesu smiled and shook the bowl. Taking a deep breath, Elizabeth picked up a couple of the crispies and popped them into her mouth. She chewed quickly, without breathing, so she could minimize the taste. But then she realized . . . it wasn't half bad. In fact, it tasted quite delicious.

"That's good!"

"Anesu tell missus so."

They continued eating until the *sadza* and crispies were gone. Picking her teeth with the tip of a knife, Anesu jerked her head toward the back of the hut, some kind of signal to Turu. He jumped up and returned with a small, scarred wooden box, placed it in front of Anesu, and sat back down. She reached in, held up a closed hand, shut her eyes, and began to chant. Elizabeth glanced at Turu for a clue about what was happening. But his eyes were also closed.

She became aware of a pulsing in the air. Eyes darting between the two of them, she waited. What was going on?

After what seemed like an age, Anesu stopped chanting, opened her hand, and held it out toward Elizabeth. There in her palm lay a mottled, chocolate-colored stone, carved in the image of an owl with a fierce golden eye that stared straight at Elizabeth.

"For missus," Anesu said.

Elizabeth clapped. "Honestly?"

Anesu threaded a hide tie through a hole in the top of the little owl, tied it off, and then, placing it to one side, held out her other hand. At first Elizabeth didn't know what she wanted. But then it dawned on her. Anesu wanted her amulet back.

Feeling a pang of sorrow, Elizabeth reached up and clasped the little stone bird that had been her companion for what seemed a lifetime. Her fingers slipped over the smooth curves of the soapstone in an old familiar pattern, her thumb sliding into the groove around the stone eye. Her friend. Her powerful friend. She would really miss its reassuring presence.

But it was time to give it back.

Elizabeth took off the amulet and handed it to Anesu. "Goodbye, little bird."

The old woman received her amulet back solemnly, with both hands, and bowed her head. They sat quietly for a moment. Then, motioning for Elizabeth to lean forward, she slipped the hide tie over her head, patted the little owl against her chest, and sat back with a pleased smile.

Elizabeth gazed down at the owl. The hide band was just the right length. The bird nestled just so against her chest. She reached up and ran her fingers over its smooth surface and found she could easily slip her thumbnail around the eye like she had with Anesu's amulet. She already felt connected to it.

"Anesu make special for missus so missus remember—"

"Oh, I would *never* have forgotten."

"Listen to Anesu. *Nadira* is to help missus remember magic *here*." Anesu laid her healed hand over Elizabeth's heart.

Elizabeth looked down at Anesu's hand, wishing she knew what the old woman meant.

Anesu dropped her hand. "When it is time, missus will understand. Amai Vedu will teach missus. But for now, remember one thing, magic is in missus's heart, not in *nadira.*"

Elizabeth stared at Anesu in dismay. "It's not magic?"

Anesu smiled. "Maybe a little."

"Oh, good, I mean, I-I'd love it anyway, even if it wasn't magic . . ." A sudden realization struck her. "Oh no! My mom's going to have a fit if I come home with this new amulet. She'll definitely notice. What am I going to tell her?"

"Missus will know what to say."

"But you don't know my mother—"

"Ssh." Anesu pressed a finger to her lips and rose to her feet.

Motioning for Elizabeth and Turu to do the same, she took each of their hands in hers, and brought them together. Elizabeth looked down at her white skin against their dark. Everything she'd ever learned about the differences between blacks and whites flashed through her mind, and she felt a momentary awkwardness. But then she became aware of how committed and strong Turu's grasp felt, and Anesu's, how warm and comforting. Elizabeth melted into the moment.

"Amai Vedu say that missus and Sabata are special to Africa, to both our peoples," Anesu said. "Change is coming, some good, some not so good. But Sabata and missus are part of it. The bwanas are wrong. Karari was wrong too. Missus and Sabata are the new way. Sabata knows all the old magic and missus will bring the new magic." She released their hands and touched each of their amulets. "Not here." She tapped their hearts. "But here."

"But what about you?" Elizabeth asked.

"Anesu's time has gone. Missus and Sabata are the future. But Anesu will always be with you both."

"Will I ever see you again?"

Anesu shook her head.

Tears pricked Elizabeth's eyelids. This was all too much. She didn't know what was expected of her. She met Turu's gaze and could see he felt the same way. She reached for her amulet and rubbed it. It felt warm to the touch.

"I'd . . . I guess I'd better go," she said.

"Turu will take missus back."

"By the way, what were those crispy little things?"

Anesu turned to Turu, her eyes twinkling. "Show missus."

"Come." He headed out the door. She followed him to the tree at the side of the hut. He stared up at the leaves for a moment, then pointed. "See, missi?"

"Leaves? But how did—"

"No, missi." Clucking his tongue, Turu stood on tiptoe, reached up, and scooped something off the leaf.

Elizabeth suddenly realized what he was doing.

"Worms!" She spat and wiped her mouth with the back of her hand. "Bloody hell, I just ate a bunch of horrible, slimy worms."

Turu opened his hand.

She shut her eyes. "No, I don't want to see it. Take it away." She opened one eye.

Turu grinned and stuffed the worm in his pocket. "Missi liked worms. Turu saw."

A low rumble echoed across the veld, and a mass of dark clouds appeared from nowhere. And then, as if someone had overturned a lake, the rain came down. Paralyzed for a moment by the force of the torrent, Elizabeth and Turu stared at each other before rushing for cover. As they charged toward the hut, golden shafts of sun streamed through the clouds and rain.

"Monkey's wedding!" Elizabeth said as she ducked into the hut.

Anesu handed Elizabeth a threadbare towel. "Eh?"

Running in behind Elizabeth, Turu rattled off something in Shona, ending with the words, "monkey's wedding." Handing him a towel, Anesu said something. He answered with a shrug, and they both looked over at Elizabeth.

Drying herself, Elizabeth glanced from Turu's amused expression to Anesu's pitying one. Her face blazed. "You're going on about monkey's wedding, is that it? Well, it's just something we say, you know like . . . well, like . . . oh, never mind."

Anesu shook her head. She held out an old snuff tin with a smile. "Take this *muti* for *picannin* bwana. Your mother will be happy to have it."

"Thank you." Elizabeth slipped the tin into her pocket, wondering how on earth she was going to explain how she got this new batch of *muti*.

Her throat suddenly felt tight. She concentrated on folding Anesu's towel. Swallowing hard, she handed the towel back to Anesu and cleared her throat. "Well, I suppose this is good-bye then. Um, thank you for the nice lunch and the amulet. I'll try and do everything you said."

Anesu nodded.

Turu started out the hut, and Elizabeth followed him. But then, halfway across the clearing, she ran back and flung her arms around Anesu's waist. And with tears running down her cheeks, she broke away and started back across the clearing. Giving the fire a wide berth, she headed for Turu, waiting at the bottom of the rise. At the top, she wiped away her tears and turned to wave one last time to Anesu, who stood watching them from the hut's doorway.

"Good-bye!" Elizabeth called, fingering her amulet.

Anesu waved.

Elizabeth and Turu walked in a comfortable silence past the black monkey thorn tree and down the other side of the ridge. She looked around. She would miss the veld. She would miss the first rains that would bring flowers and new growth. She would miss her trips with Turu to van Zyl's shop, swiping sherbit and burying "secrets" beside the baobab. She would miss trying to get Turu's wire car to run smoothly.

But perhaps most of all, she would miss the unspoken understanding and affection that only now she realized had developed between her and Turu over the years.

She slid a sidelong glance at him. He turned and grinned. She grinned back. And then they were both running across the veld, neck and neck. Arms and legs pumping, they charged over the uneven scrub, past the prickly bush, and up and over the next rise toward the Shona ruins. Just like old times. Her breath burned in her throat, and a trickle of sweat ran into one eye.

Brushing it away, she dug in and ran past him. "Beat you!"

"*Aikona!*" He zipped past her just as they reached the path to van Zyl's. He slowed down. This was where he would have to turn around. She charged past him.

"I win!" She lifted her arms in victory and then bent over to catch her breath.

"Missi always cheat," he said, through gasps.

"Uh-uh. Fair and square."

He rolled his eyes.

She glanced around. "Well, I'd better go. Don't want them to come looking for me again, hey?"

He nodded, but she could tell his mind was elsewhere. His face grew serious. "Does missi believe what Grandmother say about Turu and missi?"

She stared at him, glad he was being so direct, but not sure what to say. All that stuff Anesu had said about them being special to Africa: the new way, she said. It made her head spin. But she trusted Anesu and she did believe in magic, so she gave an uncertain nod.

Turu lifted his chin as if what she said confirmed his own thoughts on the matter. "Grandmother also say Turu and missi will see each other again."

"Honestly?"

"Grandmother tell Turu that."

Elizabeth stared at him. Was he making that up, like it was a friendly thing to do? "That would be nice, hey?"

He nodded.

"Well, then . . . bye-bye."

"Bye-bye." He turned to go.

She grinned to herself. He'd never actually said good-bye before. It was always a lift of the chin, if anything at all. Turning, she headed toward the sisal plot and the path running behind their house. She turned to wave one last time.

Turu was already gone.

For a moment she stared at the empty horizon, feeling lost and lonely. She sighed and reached up to clasp her new amulet. Her mother's frowning face rose up before her. She felt a momentary pang of anxiety but then tossed back her head. No matter. She was not giving up her little owl. She *would* find the right words to persuade her mother.

"Come, little owl. What do I tell Mom?"

THE END

Acknowledgements

Thank you to Violet, Leffy, and Tennis, and all those Africans who worked for us, whose service I didn't appreciate at the time, and whose children became my sometimes back-lane best friends.

About the Author:

Rossandra White, a fourth generation South African, grew up in Nkana, Zambia, and for a short while lived in Zimbabwe, where her novel, Monkey's Wedding, is set. Family holidays were either trips down to South Africa to visit family, over the border into the Congo or trips up to East Africa accompanied by Corky, the parrot.

She lives in Laguna Beach with her two Staffordshire Bull Terriers with whom she fights for space in her bed. When she's not writing, she's at the gym or hiking the hills behind her home in Laguna canyon.

Find out more by visiting www.rossandrawhite.com

Follow Rossandra on twitter at
www.twitter.com/RossandraWhite

Join Rossandra on Faceboook at
https://www.facebook.com/RossandraWhiteauthorpage/

Add yourself to Rossandra's mailing list at
http://eepurl.com/hRX4-/

You can learn how *Monkey's Wedding* came about on Rossandra's
website here:
http://rossandrawhite.com/how-monkeys-wedding-came-about/

If you like this book,
Please share your experience here at Amazon.com:
https://www.amazon.com/dp/B01MSSORTS/